F. G. Wood is a former teacher and consultant. Much of her career has been spent in the Middle East where, in the last ten years, she has devoted her time to early years education. Having gained a master's degree, she developed a passion for inclusive education and has worked setting up achievement centres within nurseries. Now settled back in the UK, she devotes her time to writing, where she encapsulates much of experiences of her travels into her work for young children.

For James and Annabel, with love.

F. G. Wood

QUEST FOR THE ISLAND'S TREASURE

AUSTIN MACAULEY PUBLISHERS™

LONDON • CAMBRIDGE • NEW YORK • SHARJAH

A CIP catalogue record for this title is available from the British Library.

ISBN 9781398400702 (Paperback)
ISBN 9781398400719 (ePub e-book)

www.austinmacauley.com

First Published (2021)
Austin Macauley Publishers Ltd
25 Canada Square
Canary Wharf
London
E14 5LQ

My thanks firstly goes to my dear friend, Sally Bahia, who made me realise that I could achieve whatever I set out to do. Thanks must also go to my colleague and friend, Mukami Makau, who patiently read my work and urged me to publish it. My gratitude also goes to Bethan and Niamh Kelly, two very special little girls, who unknowingly gave me encouragement. Sincere thanks also to my trusted friend and travel companion, Marian Morley, who came to Jersey with me and unwittingly gave me inspiration. Lastly, thanks to Austin Macauley Publishers who have provided encouragement and made the process for me, as a first-time author, so straightforward.

Chapter 1

It was the first day of the summer holidays and Ella stood looking out of her bedroom window as the rain lashed against the glass and formed little rivulets that cascaded down to the sill. *I am bored already,* she thought. *Whatever am I going to do for the next six weeks let alone today if the weather is going to be like this?*

Ella went down to breakfast. Her father and brother were already seated at the table, her father had his head in a newspaper and her older brother, Tom, was texting someone.

"Please put that thing away at the table," said her mother reproachfully. "This is not the time or the place to be texting."

Tom finished what he was doing and slid the mobile into his jeans pocket. He was Ella's older brother and at seventeen thought he was far better than anyone else. As far as Ella was concerned, he was a real pain. He was always saying something rude or horrible to her or was simply just annoying.

"Ah!" he exclaimed as she sat down. "The little wasp has risen at long last," he added with a smirk.

Ella ignored him and gratefully took a piece of toast her mother offered her.

Ella's mother joined them at the table. "More tea, Henry?" she asked. A grunt came from behind the newspaper. "I'll take that as a yes," she said raising her eyebrows.

The newspaper came down with a snap and Ella's father appeared as always rather grumpy first thing in the morning. Handing over his mug, he murmured, "Have you explained to Ella what is happening this week?"

"Not yet, I haven't had the chance," replied Ella's mother.

"What is happening?" Ella said, looking quite startled.

"You're being sent away finally," added Tom with a huge grin on his face. "We are all fed up with you so it is better you leave."

"That is not so," snapped Ella's mum. "Please be quiet for heaven's sake; if you can't say anything nice, keep your lips firmly closed," she added. Tom sat back still with a grin on his face.

Looking at Ella, she smiled kindly and added that no one was sending her away, and no one was fed up with her. The fact was that Grandpa Harvey, Ella's mother's dad, was coming out of hospital. Six weeks ago, he had fallen and broken his hip. He was eighty-two and needed nursing, which meant that he would be staying with them as Ella's mum was a nurse and could take care of him. It also meant her mother would have no time to spend with her. As Ella's two best friends had already gone on holiday with their parents and her father was off on a business trip, her mother wondered whether she would like to stay with Aunt Lucy on the island of Jersey.

Ella sat open mouthed when she heard this.

Aunt Lucy was her mum's older sister who Ella had not seen since she was a baby so didn't know her at all. Aunt Lucy had invited her and Tom but as he had managed to get himself a holiday job, he did not require being entertained.

Her mother quickly added that Aunt Lucy and her husband, Uncle Josh, had a potato farm on Jersey and would love to have her stay. They did not have any children of their own but had a large farmhouse in the countryside, and it would be an experience to go to Jersey, somewhere different and new.

"You can spend your day picking potatoes," said Tom grinning cheekily.

"Be quiet, Tom," barked Ella's father.

Ella was dumbfounded, why hadn't her parents asked her if she would like to go instead of just going ahead and arranging it. She knew her mother was only trying to be kind but at nearly thirteen, she felt she should be able to have a say in what she did.

Ella looked at her mother. "It sounds very nice but I hardly know Aunt Lucy."

"Oh, she is very happy to have you. In fact, it was her idea that you should go," said her mother.

Ella sat quietly thinking, Aunt Lucy maybe mum's older sister but she could be very different to her mother. What was she going to do in the countryside all day?

Tom sat opposite her at the table still smirking as he drank his coffee. Ella felt like giving him a hard kick from under the table but knew that would cause a problem so she just glared at him.

Mum explained she was booked on a flight to Jersey tomorrow so she had better start putting together what she wanted to take.

Ella had no time to object, part of her wanted to cry but knowing her brother was watching her, she said nothing and finished her breakfast in silence.

How would you feel if you discovered you were going to stay with a relative you did not know?
Would you refuse to go or would you think this maybe was an exciting opportunity?
How would this affect you?

Chapter 2

The following day was hectic packing essential clothes and toiletries for her journey and of course her small stuffed rabbit, Horace, who went everywhere with her. When it came time to leave, Ella felt rather sad and tearful. It was the fear of the unknown; what if she did not like her aunt, what if there was nothing to do there. She went to join her mother in the car.

"Peace at last," mocked Tom. "I hope you haven't forgotten Horace," he yelled after her.

Ella felt a lump in her throat, but thinking on the bright side, she realised at least she would not have to put up with her brother for a few weeks that was for sure.

Her mother took her to Cardiff Airport where they met up with a lovely, helpful and friendly air stewardess. As Ella was only twelve, she had to travel as an unaccompanied minor on the flight. This meant the air stewardess would see her onto the plane and watch out for her during the flight and then hand her over to her aunt who would meet her, all being well, in St Helier, the capital of Jersey.

Ella's mum gave her a bag to give to her aunt and made her promise to Face Time or call as soon as she could when she arrived. She kissed her and gave her a hug before Ella left to sit in the departure lounge with the stewardess.

Sitting in a comfortable seat watching the planes through the large glass windows, Ella began to feel a bit better. It was quite exciting to be travelling on your own and she suddenly felt very grown up. The stewardess could not have been nicer and did not treat her like a child. She told Ella to call her Pat and gave her the boarding pass. When it was time to board the aircraft, she escorted Ella to her seat and helped her fasten her seat belt whilst explaining it was a very short flight and if she needed anything; either she or her colleague would be ready to help. Pat left her then with a magazine to look at.

While she was waiting for the flight to take off, a young boy came to sit next to her. He introduced himself as James and explained he lived in Jersey and was travelling back home as he had been staying with his Grandparents in Wales. He was also travelling as an unaccompanied minor as he was thirteen years old. Ella explained why she was going to Jersey and how she was a bit worried about what it was going to be like. James explained Jersey was really quite a small island, but he loved it, after all, it was his home. He had been born, and now lives, in a village near the town of St Martin. He had made this flight on his own several times before.

It wasn't long before the captain announced that the flight was ready to depart and with all the doors closed, the aircraft slowly began to taxi towards the runway. Ella had flown herself several times before as she had been to Spain and France with her parents, so was familiar with the procedures. On reaching the runway, the aircraft stopped and revved its engines before lurching forward and speeding ahead. Its nose pointed upwards and in no time at all the wheels had left the ground and they were airborne.

Pat returned and handed James and Ella a bottle of orange juice and a Danish pastry each, and informed them that the flight was only fifty-five minutes so it would not be long before they would be descending. Ella enjoyed the refreshments and looked out of the window to see the English coastline disappear behind them as they started to cross the English Channel. She chatted to James who pointed out the other islands as they flew overhead. The largest one was Jersey he told her, before that lay Guernsey, Aldernay and then Sark, which was the smallest island of them all and one where there were no cars.

Ella felt her ears suddenly pop as the plane began its descent to St Helier's airport below. In no time at all the aircraft had landed smoothly on the tarmac and Pat was there ready to escort her and James to the arrivals area to collect their luggage. There was no passport control for them as The Channel Islands is part of Great Britain.

Once they had both retrieved their bags, Pat took them through the security barrier and into the arrivals hall. James waved madly at a woman in a royal blue short-sleeved dress who had long blond wavy hair; she waved back and smiled broadly. "That's my mum," he said. "Have a good holiday," he added and raced over to her, falling into her arms. Ella watched as a man joined them in a pair of stone coloured trousers and dark green Lacoste shirt. Ella guessed that was his dad. He ruffled James's hair and then James turned to Ella and pointed her out to his parents. Ella smiled and waved back.

"Ella?" said a voice enquiringly.

Ella spun round. There before her stood an older version of her mother with dark wavy hair and a warm friendly smile. Ella liked her instantly. "Aunt Lucy," she said smiling back. Aunt Lucy gave her a big hug and turned to thank Pat. She in turn wished Ella a great stay and said farewell.

Aunt Lucy looked at Ella. "I am going to say something you may not like," she said with a grin. "You are the image of your mum." Ella smiled; she didn't mind being told that as she had heard it many times before.

"Well," said Ella, "I must also look a bit like you as I think you look just like my mum."

"Really," said Aunt Lucy with a smile. "She is quite a bit younger than me so I will take that as a compliment."

They made their way out to the car park, Aunt Lucy carrying Ella's heavy suitcase. "You must be exhausted," said Aunt Lucy. "Let's get you home so you can get something to eat." Ella explained she had eaten on the plane, but Aunt Lucy was busy fishing out her car keys from her large handbag that was on her shoulder and didn't answer. There was a sudden click and a peep and the lights flashed on a battered old Range Rover, which was standing waiting to transport them to the farm. It was quite old and very muddy, but it was comfy inside with plenty of room for everything. Aunt Lucy let Ella sit next to her in the front and off they sped. As they drove away, Aunt

Lucy explained how delighted she was to have Ella to stay and how she hoped she would have a great time on Spud End Farm.

Have you ever travelled anywhere by yourself?
How would you feel or how did you feel flying somewhere all by yourself?
Do you look like someone in your family?

Chapter 3

They drove through the busy streets of St Helier and Ella peered out of the car window seeing all the familiar shops from home, Accessorize, Boots, M&S, and even Costa Coffee.

Her aunt plied her with questions about the family as they drove on and she took time to tell her all about the farm.

Soon the busy streets gave way to rolling hills and beautiful countryside with bushes and trees in every shade of green imaginable, it was all very different from Ella's home. They sped along a coast road on the east side of the island for about ten kilometres then turning left they headed inland where the fields were surrounded by high hedgerows and the buildings became few and far between. The roads changed into country lanes only wide enough to let one vehicle pass. Eventually, Aunt Lucy turned sharply left, through a rusty old gate, up a rough farm track and headed towards a large house in the distance. Pulling up sharply outside the front door, she announced, "Here we are, Spud End." Ella was amazed, as she couldn't quite believe where she was. It was so different from her home. She got out of the car and stood listening to the silence. Away in the distance she could hear a bird tweeting. The air was scented with the fragrance of flowers and grasses, insects hummed and buzzed faintly as they flew by and a butterfly silently danced amongst the shrubs growing on the garden wall. Ella was struck by the peaceful surroundings it was as if no one lived here at all.

"Come along in," said Aunt Lucy. "Your Uncle Josh is around somewhere," she continued. Ella got one of her bags and followed Aunt Lucy inside. The house was cool and had a fresh smell of lavender. They passed from the open hallway into a large lounge. The furniture was mainly made of pinewood and fashioned in a cottage style. There was a large comfortable couch richly covered in a red and cream floral print, as were the curtains. Pictures and paintings that decorated the walls were all of country scenes or animals such as deer and pheasants. Not exactly Ella's taste or her parents' but none the less it was clean, tidy and very welcoming.

"Hello," shouted a cheerful voice from an open doorway. Ella looked to her right and there stood a rugged faced man with a beaming smile on his face. His sleeves were rolled up and his shirt half open displaying a dark hairy sun-tanned chest. His eyes twinkled and he held out his right hand saying, "Hi, I'm your Uncle Josh, come through." Ella shook his hand and followed him into a large kitchen. There were two other men standing drinking a glass of beer. Uncle Josh handed Ella a glass of cloudy lemonade.

"This is Art and Jed who work here on the farm," said Aunt Lucy. Both men nodded a greeting. "So where is my lemonade?" she exclaimed. "It's thirsty work collecting nieces from the airport." She grinned. Uncle Josh poured her a tall glassful with pieces of lemon and ice. "My own recipe," she said winking at Ella. Ella sipped it gratefully. It was delicious, sweet and tangy as it was laced with ginger.

" Now," said Aunt Lucy, "Josh will get the rest of your luggage from the car and then we'll go upstairs to your room and you can freshen up and then we can all have something to eat. You must be hungry after your long journey."

Ella drained her glass and was then taken up two sets of rickety stairs to the attic room. Aunt Lucy explained no one had used this room for years, but she had cleaned it out especially for Ella's stay. It was a large room, almost half the house and it had a window under the rafters. Ella had to bend down in order to look out of it. The ceiling was actually the roof so it sloped down on both sides. There was a large bed with lots of pure white pillows and a cornflower blue duvet cover. Next to that was a wicker table with a lamp on, which had a bright pink shade. Ella spied a large wardrobe at one end of the room and an old-fashioned chest of drawers at the other. There was a strange looking wicker chair with a fan shaped backrest and an oak blanket chest. This room was a lot bigger than Ella's own bedroom back home and it was all quite over-whelming, but she smiled at her aunt who then led her down one set of rickety stairs to where the other bedrooms were and showed her a small shower room, which was for her to use.

"Thank you," she said gratefully. "I'll freshen up then come down."

Fifteen minutes later, they were all sitting at a large pine rectangular table in the kitchen. Art and Jed sat opposite Ella and her Uncle and Aunt sat either end. The back door suddenly opened and in came a young woman with red hair and a broad Scottish accent. "I'm not late, am I?" she said.

"Not at all, in fact you are bang on time as I am just about to dish up," replied Aunt Lucy. Sit yourself down next to Ella, my niece who I have been telling you about. The young woman came straight over to Ella and kissed her on both cheeks.

"Hi, I'm Jenny; it is great to finally meet you," she said. "I have heard so much about you from Lucy. How was your journey?" she added.

Ella told her how she had met a boy called James on the flight and how she had been well looked after by Pat a friendly air stewardess. Jenny then explained that she had only lived in Jersey for nine months. She had married Art last November and they lived in a cottage on the farm estate. She had been lucky to find a job at the local health centre and was now the community nurse.

Aunt Lucy placed an enormous dish of lasagne on the table and a bowl of carrots and broccoli. There was fresh crusty bread and butter as well. Ella tucked in heartily.

After supper, Jenny explained she had to work the next day but would be free the following day to take Ella out. Her and Art had just acquired a puppy, in fact it was a golden retriever who was very excitable and needed a lot of walking. She said she would like to show Ella some of the lovely places on the island. Aunt Lucy also explained that it was a very busy time of the year for them, as they had to harvest the potatoes. Ella could willingly help, but as this was her first real trip to Jersey, she should really explore her new environment. Aunt Lucy promised that every day either she or Jenny would do something with her so she would always have something to look forward to. Ella thought that sounded great. She would not have had this at home. Keen to investigate her new environment, she thought it was a good idea to get to know her surroundings first. That night she went up to bed feeling quite excited at the prospect of her stay on the island of Jersey.

Do you think you would like the countryside compared to city?

Have you ever stayed in a strange house or slept in a strange bed?

Ella appears to like her new environment, why do you think that is?

Chapter 4

After a hearty breakfast of cereal and scrambled eggs on toast [which tasted wonderful to Ella, much better than her breakfast at home], Ella decided to go for a walk.

Uncle Josh gave her a mobile phone and explained that she only had to press one number to speed dial him.

"I am not allowed to have a mobile," said Ella.

"I understand your parents do not want you to have a mobile all the time, but this is just for you to use while you are staying here, so if you get lost, we can find you easily. Jersey is a small island and we want to know where you are when you are by yourself, okay?"

Ella agreed and slipped it into the pocket of her shorts. "That reminds me," said Ella, "I forgot to call Mum when I arrived."

"Don't worry I called her last night, she knows you've arrived safely, you can speak to her this evening," said Aunt Lucy.

Aunt Lucy then gave Ella a little map of the surrounding area and directed her to a small forest on the left-hand side of the farmhouse. Thanking her, Ella set off to explore with a small bottle of water.

Once she got to the edge of the forest, Ella followed a narrow winding path that lead through the forest undergrowth. Overhead, the trees shaded the way and provided the air with a scented aroma from their many different leaves. Wild flowers and grasses grew either side of the path tickling her legs as she passed by. Dandelions, Daisies, Campion and Speedwell, their colours enriching the ground she trod. Ella thought how different this was from where she lived in the city. It is all so beautiful with the many shades of greens and other hues that were dazzling in the morning sunlight. There was a light breeze, but otherwise it was quite warm.

The pathway suddenly gave way to a field of lavender, which not only displayed remarkable colours of blue, purple, lilac and mauve but also filled the air with a rich fragrant scent that made Ella feel quite soporific. Ella touched the plants gently as she walked along the side catching the smell with her fingertips.

At the end of the field, there was a road, not a main road of course, more like a country lane. Ella looked both ways and as there was nothing coming, she crossed to the other side. Almost opposite was an opening in the hedgerow. Ella squeezed through to see a pathway ahead. *That must lead somewhere,* she thought and proceeded along the over grown route. After a few metres, the pathway narrowed and the trees and shrubs either side had grown overhead forming a covered archway. It was almost like entering a tunnel that was formed with leaves. Tiny openings above let through rays of sunlight.

A little further on, the tunnel opened into a small circular area, which had a formation of large grey stones. All around there was a thick hedgerow that encased the stones. Looking closely, Ella saw they formed a pattern. Walking around to the left side, she noticed that the stones, which were about a metre high, formed a corridor, which led to a ring of larger stones that had a huge stone covering them. It almost looked like a pathway to a little stone house. Someone had strewn rose petals at the entrance and there were bunches of wild flowers placed in the corridor. What was strange was that there was a rosy red apple placed on top of one of the large stones at the side.

"Quite amazing isn't it?" said a voice.

Ella nearly jumped out of her skin but managed to turn round with her heart thumping in her chest. There at the end of the tunnel she had just come through, stood an old man. He was neatly dressed in a pair of jeans and a pale blue shirt. His sleeves were rolled up and he carried what looked like a thin branch as a staff. His arms and face were well suntanned, which made his white hair and beard stand out. His gold-rimmed glasses sat loosely on the end of his nose. He smiled at Ella and then called out, "Hey, Martha, come and see who is here."

With a rustle an older lady appeared. She had a pair of khaki shorts and a pink T-shirt on. What looked like a rain mac was tied round her waist and a funny cloche hat sat on her head. A rather strange smile crept across her face. She was also carrying a staff and looked very suntanned. Ella felt a bit uneasy.

"Hello, dear," she said warmly. "Have you come to admire the tombs?"

"Tombs?" said Ella.

"Oh, yes, dear," she continued. "This is an ancient burial ground that has been here for thousands of years."

Ella was not sure about all this. Looking around, she noticed strange things hanging from the trees. They were sorts of mobiles crudely made with shells and tied together with different coloured ribbons. Suddenly, she thought she didn't want to be here anymore.

"I am really sorry," she said. "I didn't mean to touch anything."

She walked towards the couple who were by the entrance to the tunnel and said, "I really have to go, my parents are waiting for me." With that as quick as a flash, she raced past them and sped back down the tunnel and didn't stop till she came to the road.

Meanwhile, the elderly couple looked at each other and chuckled strangely, then suddenly, with a nod to each other, they slowly started to shrink until they merged into the long grass. They were no longer people but had changed their form and now slithered away silently as two thin mottled green coloured grass snakes.

Would you be brave enough to go off by yourself?
What would you hope to find in the countryside?
Do you think Ella had the right reaction to the strangers she met?

Is it a good thing to chat to people we don't know, even if they do seem friendly?

Chapter 5

Ella's heart was still pumping furiously in her chest as she reached the field of lavender. She swept through it, the scent from the plants making her feel quite giddy. She slowed down a bit when she got to the forest track, looking round she spied no one and stopped to catch her breath. Feeling nervous once again, she continued quickly on her way and it wasn't long before the forest gave way to open fields, which was Spud End and there in the distance was the farmhouse. *Thank heavens I am here*, she thought. Ella could not explain why she felt so frightened or why it was that when she saw the strangers, she felt the need to run away. Maybe she was over reacting, as this was an unfamiliar place to her.

As she entered through the back door, Aunt Lucy was busy preparing lunch and had her back to her. Ella managed a breathless "Hi."

"Oh, hello, dear," said Aunt Lucy warmly when Ella walked in, "did you have a nice walk?" When she looked round at Ella, she was quite surprised. "Gosh are you alright?" she added.

"I'm fine," said Ella. "I have just been running that's all."

"Well you must be hungry then with all that exercise," replied Aunt Lucy promptly. "Wash your hands and help yourself to a sandwich or two, there is ham, cheese and egg, there are also some ripe plums and plenty of lemonade, so tuck in."

Ella did as she was told and sat down at the table. She helped herself to a ham salad sandwich with tangy pickle in it. The bread was fresh, crusty on the outside and really soft inside and with the ham salad filling it just tasted delicious.

"Why does everything taste so much better here?" she asked.

"Does it really?" laughed her aunt. "I'm glad to see you have a good appetite and enjoy your food."

Her aunt came to join her at the table with a large mug of steaming tea.

"Let's tuck in before the men get here," she said. "It is almost their lunch time."

They sat enjoying what Ella thought was a feast, in silence for a few minutes, then Aunt Lucy asked Ella where she had been. Ella mentioned she had strolled through the forest and into the lavender field. Her aunt explained the field belonged to their neighbour and he allowed her to pick as much of the blooms as she wanted. *That explains the lovely fragrance of the herb when I walked into the house*, thought Ella.

Ella then asked her aunt if there were any tombs nearby. Aunt Lucy was surprised by her question. She told Ella there was a small graveyard attached to the church in the village, which had one large tomb as she could recall, but that was for a family that lived in the parts over a hundred years ago. She was not aware of any other tombs nearby. Aunt Lucy then changed the subject asking Ella if she would like to come into St Helier with her that afternoon. Aunt Lucy had to pick up something in town and she thought Ella might like to see the glass church. Ella had visions of a church made out of glass and was keen to see this unusual sight.

They finished off their lunch and just as they were about to leave, Uncle Josh, Jed and Art appeared looking tired and dirty. "Just what the doctor ordered," said Uncle Josh as he washed his hands. "I'm starving."

"There's a fresh pot of tea there so help yourselves," said Aunt Lucy. "And mind you clear up after you," she added with a grin.

She explained that she was taking Lucy to see the glass church in St Helier and to pick up the part for the old potato picker, which meant they would not be back until around five. She than mentioned that they would eat at The Jersey Royal that evening. Aunt Lucy explained to Ella that this was the

25

pub in the village and it served very nice meals. Uncle Josh nodded in agreement and said he would be ready around six.

Twenty minutes later, Ella and Aunt Lucy had become part of the busy traffic on the outskirts of St Helier. Aunt Lucy explained there was one problem living in a beautiful place and that was the tourists, especially this time of year. Ella asked her how she came to live in Jersey. Her aunt explained that she had been working as a nurse when one day a young man came in to the ward after he had nearly drowned in a sailing accident. That had been Uncle Josh. He had been on holiday in Wales and capsized his small sailing boat in rough seas. Once he recovered from the trauma, they started to see each other and then one night after they had been out to a disco, Uncle Josh asked her to marry him. The rest is history she added. Uncle Josh's father owned Spud End and his father before him. As Uncle Josh had no brothers, it was only natural that he would take it on. Aunt Lucy came to visit the family and fell in love not only with Uncle Josh but also with the island of Jersey. Ella thought that was lovely, she had not realised both her mother and aunt were nurses.

They stopped briefly at a large warehouse and Aunt Lucy disappeared inside for a few minutes then reappeared with a large box, which a young man helped her place in the boot of the car. They then sped off along the coast road. Ella could see a castle that appeared to be out at sea, but Aunt Lucy explained that was Elizabeth Castle and at low tide you could walk out to it.

They drove around the bay; Ella admired the blue sea and the soft sandy beach. Aunt Lucy turned right along a narrow road and then after a short distance, she pulled up in front of a church. "Here we are," she announced. "The glass church."

"But it is not made of glass," said Ella.

"Come and see," beckoned Aunt Lucy.

Ella walked through the open doorway and could not quite believe her eyes. The church had the most beautiful glass panels in the wooden doors. The panels were not coloured but were made of opaque glass and the designs were exquisite. On the door to the church were two plaques of what Ella thought were angels with their arms crossed over their chests. Their faces were etched so finely on the glass panel. Aunt Lucy opened the doors to reveal the church itself. Lucy, initially, was dazzled by the brightness. At the main altar, there was a cross and this had beautiful flowers etched all around it. Ella walked forward to get a closer view and noticed the altar rail was all in glass too. There was another side altar with more of these angels with their arms crossed. The whole church was full of light and Ella got a strange sensation of wonder as she looked around her. There was an opaque glass object, about a metre or so high that was just by the entrance. It stood out, as the glass appeared to be in strips. Ella asked her aunt what it was and she told her it was the baptismal font. This beautiful glass font held the water to baptise or christen babies. Ella particularly liked the door panels in the church entrance, which had a simple leaf design, but again in the opaque glass the light appeared translucent through the window panels.

"It is lovely, isn't it?" asked her aunt.

"No," said Ella. "I think it is absolutely fabulous, like an ice palace."

Aunt Lucy smiled and explained that the glass was designed and made by a Frenchman called Rene Lalique. This was a long time ago in the 1930s. He knew a woman called Lady Trent who in fact was the wife of Mr Boots the chemist. She had paid for all the work to be done when her husband passed away as a memorial to him. Rene Lalique is world renowned for his enamel jewellery, perfume bottles and beautiful glassware. Ella just thought it was wonderful, unlike anything she had seen before.

Going back in the car, Ella thought how much she had seen and done and had not yet been here two days, she certainly was so glad she had come to visit.

When you go to someone else's house, does the food taste better there?
Did you think it was strange that Aunt Lucy did not know about the tombs?

Do you like seeing unusual things?
Would you have been as delighted as Ella to visit such an unusual church?

Chapter 6

That evening, Aunt Lucy, Uncle Josh and Ella all went to the Jersey Royal. It was a large pub where a jolly faced man greeted them warmly and introduced himself to Ella as Ted. He was the landlord. They took a large table as Jenny and Art were going to join them later. The table was by a window, which was lovely and bright. It was like being in someone's house as it was all very cosy. There were snug sofas, comfy armchairs and small tables scattered around the bar as well as four large dining tables by the windows. There was a huge grate that had shiny horse brasses all around it but no fire as it was too warm. Uncle Josh pointed out of the window, as coming along was Jenny and Art, but way in front on a long lead was a cute golden retriever puppy.

"I see Bailey is bringing Jenny and Art for a drink," said Uncle Josh. Aunt Lucy laughed as the little puppy was haring along tugging Jenny who was almost running.

Once they came inside, the little puppy was so pleased to see them it took several minutes to settle him down, not before he had jumped and trampled on everyone as well as licked them excitedly. Thankfully, Ella liked dogs and thought the puppy was gorgeous; they made friends instantly.

Over supper, Ella told Jenny all about her trip to the Glass church and Jenny told her that tomorrow she would take her for a walk along the coastal road with Bailey if she wanted. Ella was delighted to accept.

Later when they had finished eating, they all sat with their drinks and chatted. Ella briefly looked out of the window. Something had caught her eye, there by an old oak tree stood the two old people she had seen by the tombs. It was definitely them although they were dressed differently. They stood there with the staffs in their hand and the old man had the gold-rimmed spectacles resting on his nose and the lady had the funny cloche hat. They were looking towards her with a weird smile. Ella felt very uneasy. Her expression must have changed as her Aunt asked her what was wrong. Ella said nothing but continued to stare at the couple. All at once, they seemed to melt away into thin air.

"Who are you looking at?" said Aunt Lucy. Ella could not answer, as she was stunned. They were there, it had not been her imagination, so where were they now. Ella turned to her aunt and told her she thought she saw two people she had seen on her walk that day, but they had disappeared. "They were probably tourists," said her Aunt. "They rush around trying to see everything in a short time instead of taking it all in slowly." Ella knew this was not the case. Something was not right. Her instinct to run away from them had been correct. She hoped she would not see them again.

The next day, Jenny collected her in her Jeep and with Bailey in the back; they sped off to the coast. Jenny drove to a small car park and leaving the car, they walked down over the shingle until they found a coastal path, part of which ran along by a narrow wall. The view was lovely out over the English Channel. There was a breeze, which sent ripples across the water. Ella chatted away to Jenny and Bailey was let off the lead, as the path was narrow so he couldn't go very far. They walked around a small bay until they came to a large tower that stood out on the rocks by the sea, which Jenny said was an old fortress and was now partly painted red and white and was a navigational aid for ships. They walked around it and then Jenny spied a café a few metres away. "Time for an ice cream I think," she said. Bailey was put on the lead and they headed towards the small premises with tables and chairs outside.

Ella was asked to look after Bailey whilst Jenny went into buy the ices.

"He's a cool dog," said a familiar voice. Ella looked up to see James standing in front of her.

"Well, what are you doing here," she asked, pleased to see him.

"I live here," he said, smiling. "Had you forgotten?" Ella explained whom she was with and that they been walking along the coastal path. James told her his parents owned the bakery in the town so this was where he came most afternoons as he cycled part of the coastal path on his way to see his friend Marcus.

James and his friend had been doing some investigations he told her. Ella was intrigued. "What investigations?" she asked. He lowered his voice and said there are some strange people around. "I know," said Ella and told James about the weird couple she had seen at the tombs. She was going to tell him she saw them at the Jersey Royal pub but had to stop as Jenny was coming. Ella introduced James and Jenny kindly asked him if he wanted an ice. James thanked her but said no, as he had to get back. Ella had mentioned she had a mobile and James asked her for the number. Uncle Josh had written it in white ink on the side of the phone. James put it into his mobile and said he would call her later that day so they could arrange to meet up soon. After saying goodbye, he then cycled along the coastal path back towards the town.

Ella and Jenny sat and ate their ice creams, which were really delicious as they were made with real Jersey cream. Ella asked Jenny about the tombs. She was baffled as she had not come across any such tombs but said she knew of someone that would know. She told Ella of a lady who was a patient of hers that was ninety-three years old and had lived all her life in Jersey; in fact, she had never been off the island. If there are old tombs, Maud will know all about them, she said.

If you were Ella, would you have told your aunt and uncle about the strange couple?
How would you feel if you knew you saw something happen but knew no one would believe you?
Ella seems to want to know more about these tombs, do you think they may have a story to tell?

Chapter 7

That evening, James called as promised and his mother was able to speak to Aunt Lucy. Alison, James's mum, invited Ella and Aunt Lucy over to their home the following Friday at around 10 a.m.

Friday could not come soon enough for Ella; she was eager to hear all about James's investigations and to see if he had discovered anything since they last met.

Alison, who Ella had seen at the airport, greeted them warmly and ushered Aunt Lucy into the kitchen for a coffee while James and Ella went out into the garden. James said he wanted to tell her all about the investigation he was doing with his friend Marcus. He explained they had been out on their bikes and had gone down to the tower that Ella had seen near the coastal path. They had parked their bikes and were clambering over the rocks looking for small stones to skim over the water when they noticed a funny looking man who was going round the tower feeling the stonework. James and Marcus watched him and when he noticed them, he seemed to disappear into thin air and there in his place was a black dog. The dog barked fiercely at them so they kept well away.

"It was as if this man had changed into a dog," said James. "It was really weird."

"Was there no one with the black dog?" Ella asked.

"There didn't seem to be anyone," added James.

Ella told James about the two people she had seen and how they had seemed to disappear into thin air outside the Jersey Royal. "I think we need to investigate that also," said James. "Something strange is going on." Ella told him what Aunt Lucy had said about them being tourists who rushed around trying to see everything and maybe they had just run off. James was not convinced, as he was sure like Ella, he had seen the man just fade away.

Aunt Lucy came into the garden to say goodbye and to tell Ella she would come back around 6 p.m. to collect her, so this meant Ella had virtually the whole day to share with James. After a light lunch, James told his mother they would walk along the coastal path to the tower and meet up with Marcus. Alison added the usual about being careful and not doing anything stupid on the coastal path, as it could be very dangerous. They listened attentively then taking a bottle of water each, they left.

"She always goes on like that," said James.

"My mum's the same," said Ella.

"I don't think they realise we can look after ourselves, I am almost fourteen," added James.

Ella agreed, having a much older brother who was nowhere near as sensible as she was made her think, that her mum should understand only too well how responsible she was.

They stepped out into brilliant sunshine and although there was a soft breeze, it certainly wasn't cold. They took the road that ran parallel to the coast and walked along facing the oncoming traffic. James led the way and eventually they turned off the road down a narrow pathway, which led them to the seashore. From here, they were able to pick up the coastal path that led round to the tower, which they could see in the distance at the end of the small bay.

The tide was going out so the rocks and stones below housed tiny rock pools, which were teeming with life although James and Ella did not see that. They were also oblivious to the sea gulls that were swooping down feasting on the crabs and other crustacean that the tide had left behind. They were far too busy trying to find reasons why people could just disappear.

The rocks looked very slippery covered in algae and seaweed and Ella in particular walked tentatively making sure she kept to the narrow pathway, there was no way she wanted to slip and fall into the rocks below. James on the other hand was used to the path and kept up a brusque pace walking at times very close to the edge.

They reached the tower, which stood on a very short peninsula. There were several people around, mainly tourists, who were snapping pictures of this beautiful spot.

A voice called out to James and turning round Ella spied a red-haired boy with freckles. He had a cheeky grin on his face and a pair of spectacles that made him look very intelligent. He made his way towards them. James introduced Marcus, his close friend from school. She discovered he lived in the town with James and that they had known each other since they had been in nursery school.

James told Marcus that he had spoken to Ella about the incident with the black dog, he also mentioned Ella's story of the strange couple she had seen in a clearing. Marcus was very interested to hear that. Just like James, he was convinced something peculiar was going on and wanted to get to the bottom of it.

Marcus was intrigued by the tombs that Ella said she had seen.

"That's what the lady said they were," said Ella.

Marcus thought for a minute and then said, "You do know there are some prehistoric sites on Jersey, don't you?"

"No," said Ella.

"What makes you think what Ella saw was a prehistoric burial site?" asked James.

"Well it's just that she said the stones were arranged in a pattern that sounds to me like a prehistoric burial site. There are several on Jersey, they are called Dolmens and my dad, who's a teacher, knows all about them, he has taken me to see some of them."

"So how old are these sites and how do we know they were burial grounds, they could have been the remains of houses," said James.

"They are thousands of years old; I mean 2000 BC at least. Some of the sites were excavated and they found human bones and bits of pottery, stone tools, jewellery and other bits and pieces used probably by Stone Age man. I'd like to see the place you found, Ella, just to see if it is a Dolmen or burial site, do you think you could take us there."

"Sure," answered Ella, "but I would rather Aunt Lucy didn't know about it, she might not like me going there. I found it a bit creepy, but if you come too, I suppose it will be okay."

"Don't worry we'll protect you," Marcus said with a wink.

"Right we'll arrange it soon, for now though let's look at the tower and see if we can find what that man was looking for."

They made their way towards the tower and where they had seen the strange man a few days before. Cautiously, they made their way round the other side of the tower feeling the smooth surface of the brickwork. The structure, built out of blocks of stone, was painted in horizontal stripes of bright red and white. Marcus explained this was to ward ships away from the dangerous rocks below. They scanned the walls, looking at the brickwork to see if there was anything unusual. The stonework felt cold and damp. All appeared to be normal.

A sudden shout made them all turn around. A small group of tourists eager to get a snapshot of the tower were not impressed with the children who were appearing to hug the brickwork. They quickly moved away and took themselves off to the other side of the tower, which faced the sea.

"I don't understand it," said James puzzled.

"What do you think the man was looking for?" enquired Ella.

"I don't know," said Marcus. "He seemed to be feeling all the bricks for some reason."

"You say it was this side you saw the man, so let's have one more look here," said Ella.

As they started to feel the brickwork again around the tower, Ella's foot stepped on something that caused a scraping sound. She bent down to see what it was and picked up a small key. It wasn't a house key, but a small iron key about an inch long, with a narrow shaft and a bow at one end. The other end had a thin collar and the pin held the key wards.

"That is a lever type key and it looks fairly old," said Marcus.

"I wonder what it is from?" questioned James.

They bent down to look at the ground where Ella had found it. There didn't appear to be anything else there.

"Is there a key hole in the brickwork at all?" enquired Marcus.

"Can't see anything," said James, but as he stood up his heel pressed against the base of the tower and one of the bricks moved. James knelt down to investigate. The brick was definitely loose. He took hold of either side of the stone block and wiggled it gently from side to side. The brick began to move outwards.

"Keep a look out both of you," said James excitedly. "I think we have something here."

They did as they were asked and stood in front of James, partially hiding him from view so no one could see what he was doing. Meanwhile, James continued pulling at the loose brick and eventually managed to remove it from the wall. It revealed a very dark gap. Gingerly he put his hand inside the hole, feeling around the hole he discovered it appeared to be much bigger than the size of the brick and reaching in further his fingers touched something soft. He stretched further still and grasped hold of the soft thing that was material and pulled it out.

As soon as it had been removed from the hole, James wiggled the loose brick back into place and finally kicked it into position with his foot. Picking up the soft material, he could see it was a velvet bag. It was closed with a drawstring at one end; however, there was something small inside. It was obviously quite old, as the colour of the material had faded. As James stood up, Ella and Marcus swung round to face him.

"What have you got," Marcus enquired excitedly.

"I don't know," said James, "but something tells me we are about to find out."

Why do you think that sometimes Mums and Dads remind children of things they already know?

Would you be inquisitive and want to know why these people seem to disappear?
What do you think could be in the bag?

Chapter 8

The children made their way back to the main path leading away from the tower and went and sat under a large beech tree that was by the road. Marcus was itching to find out what was inside the bag; he took it from James and fumbled about trying to prise it open. Eventually, he was able to get his hand inside and draw out a small wooden box.

The box held a small chest with a semi-circular lid. There were brass decorations on it and a small brass lock.

"Try the key," whispered Ella.

"You have gotta be kidding," said Marcus.

James pressed the key into the lock and it appeared to fit. He turned the key anti clockwise; it didn't budge at first as it was very stiff then suddenly it gave way with a click and James was able to press the clip fastener and the lid popped open.

Inside was a folded-up piece of paper that was quite yellow with age. As James took it out, he carefully opened it up to reveal some very fancy writing.

"Can you read this?" James asked the others. "It seems it has been handwritten."

"Let me see," said Marcus. Looking over James's shoulder, he attempted to read the small fancy script. Ella looked too and together they slowly tried to decipher the words.

Treasure lies deep within the Isle
To find it all will be a trial
Seek the castle by Gorey Bay
Find the Gargoyle who knows the way
A mythical being rests inside this place
A creature you have no need to face
He guards something you will need
Seek the alcove to proceed.

"It is a treasure map of sorts," James said eagerly.

"Well, not exactly treasure," Marcus pointed out, "but it is a clue giving instructions to what we do not know."

"It says there is treasure deep within the isle," replied James.

"Is there treasure on this island?" asked Ella.

"I have heard my dad talk about treasure on Jersey but it is just a story. I do not really think it is true," replied Marcus.

"Is there a castle in Gorey Bay?" asked Ella.

Marcus read the words again. "Of course, there is a castle in Gorey Bay; it must mean Mont Orgueil or Gorey Castle in St Martins," he said. "We have to go there."

"If we do get to this castle, we have to find a gargoyle, what on earth is that?" asked Ella.

The boys looked at each other.

"No idea," said James, "but I am sure we can find out."

"I may be able to," said Ella. "I am meeting an old lady who has lived all her life here and apparently she knows everything about Jersey, I will certainly ask her about the treasure and gargoyles."

The boys looked at Ella in amazement.

"Brilliant find out as much as you can," said James.

"I'll try and ask my dad," said Marcus. "The only problem is he'll start asking me questions like why do you want to know that and then before I know it, I will tell him."

"Don't do that for heaven's sake," replied James. "This information stays between us, right?"

"Right," they all agreed.

"This could be a complete wild goose chase," said Marcus doubtfully.

"Listen," said James. "So what if it is, we don't know so we have to investigate, right?"

"Right," said Ella.

"Okay," added Marcus. "Let's go for it."

"I think we need to plan a trip to St Martins to visit Gorey Castle," said James. "I'll keep the box and clue, we tell no one else about this, okay?"

"Too right," said Ella.

With that, they made their way back to James's house.

What do you make of this clue?
Do you think there could be treasure on the island?
Would you keep it a secret or would you tell an adult about it all?

Chapter 9

A few days later, Jenny came by after lunch to take Ella to meet her patient Maud. Ella of course had already imagined what this old lady would be like. No doubt, she would be in a wheel chair and at ninety-three she could probably not see or hear very well. In fact, Ella thought she might be quite gaga.

How wrong she was. Maud might be ninety-three but she was more like someone in their seventies. She was a little old woman with grey hair, but her eyes sparkled bright and she was as sharp as a tack with all her wits about her. She remembered things from the past as if they happened yesterday; however, some things that happened yesterday she found difficult to recall. Like where she had put the book she had been reading, or when she needed to pay her electricity bill. That's where Jenny could help her out.

When Jenny and Ella arrived at Maud's cottage, she was busy in her kitchen baking. She had made some scones to have with their tea. She greeted them warmly and got them seated in her cosy sitting room where she served them tea.

She started to tell them all about Jersey during the Second World War when the Germans occupied the island for five long years. She had stories to tell of how difficult it was with little to no food and how they felt sorry for some of the very young German soldiers especially over Christmas when they missed their families even though they were the occupying forces and were the enemy.

Maud asked Ella how she found Jersey and Ella began by saying how much she enjoyed staying with her aunt and uncle and how she had met so many lovely people. She then got a chance to ask Maud if there was any treasure on the island.

"Of course, there is treasure here," she answered. "The Dolmens hold lots of treasure."

"What are the Dolmens?" asked Ella.

"Why, they are the Neolithic sites from thousands of years ago," replied Maud.

Maud explained there were several Dolmen sites on the island and that they were stones arranged in a pattern by people that lived on the island maybe four thousand years ago. These were burial sites and treasure was often buried with the dead. Ella didn't let on she knew this already but was pleased to hear that what Marcus had told her was all correct.

There is also the German's treasure.

"What is that," asked Ella, suddenly very interested.

"Oh, they hid lots of treasure here on the Island of Jersey; it was brought over in boats from France."

"Do you mean treasure as in jewels and gold?" asked Ella.

"All sorts of wonderful things they smuggled over and kept it well hidden from us islanders, that's for sure," replied Maud.

"I thought that was a myth," added Jenny.

"Certainly, isn't," replied Maud. "There's treasure here left by the Germans, that is for sure."

Jenny winked at Ella and continued to sip her tea.

Ella asked Maud about Mont Orgueil. Maud knew it by a different name she called it *lé Vièr Châté*, which meant the old castle in Jerriais. Maud explained Jerriais is the old language that the islanders on Jersey spoke. It is a form of the Norman language, so a dialect of French, although nowadays it was dying out as English was the main language spoken by everybody. She explained how they used to baffle the Germans by speaking their own language so they couldn't understand them. She could speak it fluently and was proud to do so.

"Is *lé Vièr Châté* very old?" asked Ella. Maud explained it was over 800 years old and was a medieval castle. She said it had many secrets and hidden treasures and it was where the faerie folk were reported to be as well as at the Dolmens.

"Faerie folk?" said Ella. "Who are they?"

"Have you never heard of faerie folk?" asked Maud.

"Do you mean faeries as in nymphs, elves and pixies," said Jenny.

"Indeed, I do," added Maud. "They are very real on this island."

Jenny smiled as she was not convinced about such things at all, but obviously for Maud these sort of stories were very much part of life on Jersey.

Ella was intrigued and wanted to know more about the 'faerie folk'. She asked Maud if they had wings and lived in flowers, thinking about the Fairies she had learnt about when she was very young.

"Heavens, no," said Maud. "They are as real as you and me, but they don't always want you to see them. They can come and go as quick as lightening," she added clicking her fingers, "some are very mischievous and are not always good." Softly she carried on, "They change into animals and can play tricks on you, don't meddle with the faeries whatever you do as it will bring you bad luck."

"I think it is time for us to leave now," interrupted Jenny. "I have to take Bradley out for his walk. Is there anything I can get you for tomorrow, Maud?" Jenny got up to leave; Ella was a bit disappointed, as she would like to have stayed a bit longer. Maud shook her head negatively but said she would look forward to seeing Jenny in the morning.

Ella thanked Maud for her delicious scones and said she hoped to see her soon. Maud said she would be welcome anytime, as she loved to have a bit of company. As they were leaving, Maud took Ella's arm and whispered softly in her left ear, remember this:

Faerie folk are easily found,
Listen, take note they are all around
If they need help, they will come to you
Be sure you're ready, there's plenty to do.

With that, she looked Ella in the eye and squeezing her arm, smiled gently as she left.

Ella thanked her once again and told her she would see her soon.

Ella was amazed at what she had just heard from Maud. It all sounded so incredible.

As Ella got into the car, Jenny started the engine and said, "Do not listen to a word Maud says, she is full of all sorts of stories about this and that. Treasure indeed, I hardly think the Germans would have brought treasure over from France during wartime let alone leave it here. I suppose at her age she is living in a dream world and as long as she is happy and stays healthy, it really isn't an issue. Just you put it down to the ramblings of an old woman."

Ella nodded but actually began to think about what Maud had told her and certain things started to make sense. 'They come and go as quick as lightening' that made sense to Ella. She knew she would definitely be going to see Maud again as she found what she had to say very interesting and she couldn't wait to tell the boys.

What would you make of what Maud was saying?
Who believes in Faeries nowadays?
Do you think there is any truth in what Maud says or do you think she is just rambling on as some old people are prone to do?
What do you make of it all?

Chapter 10

That evening, Ella phoned James and told him what Maud had said. He was very interested in what she had to say about the Dolmens but thought that story about faeries was a bit farfetched. He was though keener than ever to go to Gorey Castle. He told Ella he would speak to his mum and arrange for them to visit the Castle with Marcus early next week. In the meantime, he would see what information he could find out himself and get back to her soon.

As planned, Ella was able to visit Maud again with Jenny another afternoon that week. Maud was pleased to see her and as before had prepared a little tea for them. Ella and Jenny sat on her comfy sofa with a plate each of strawberries and Jersey cream. As they ate, Jenny mentioned the flower festival to Maud that was being held in Howard Davis Park the following week and how she would like to take her. Maud was thrilled with the idea and said she would certainly love to go.

Ella told Maud she was going to visit Gorey Castle. Maud chuckled.

"Watch out for the creature then," she said.

"What creature?" enquired Ella.

"The one that is flying in through the window, he holds lots of secrets."

Ella was puzzled but carried on eating her strawberries. She then asked if Maud knew anything about gargoyles.

Maud explained a gargoyle was an ugly stone statue of a creature that usually could be found around the tops of castles to ward off evil spirits. In most cases, she explained, they actually acted as a drain for the rainwater to pass through so it didn't drip down the castle walls and spoil them.

"Do you think there will be gargoyles at Gorey Castle?" asked Ella.

"For sure," answered Maud.

"You will find they are not just on the roof of the castle."

Ella was a bit puzzled but as she had never seen a gargoyle, she decided it was best not to ask anything more. She had gleaned enough information to tell the boys exactly what they had to look for.

Maud went on to tell Ella about all the places she should visit. She mentioned the glass church which Ella told her she had already seen and then the Corbiere lighthouse and the Devil's Hole and of course the sandcastle man.

"Who is the sandcastle man," enquired Ella.

Maud didn't answer as she was staring out of the window.

"Is everything alright, Maud?" Jenny asked.

"It's just they are here again, that is twice this week. What is it that they want?" Maud said to herself.

"Who?" quizzed Jenny.

"The faerie folk, did you not see them?" Maud looked at Ella.

"An old man and woman, as soon as I spy them, they disappear."

"Ah!" exclaimed Jenny very knowingly. "I am sure they'll be back."

Jenny looked at Ella and winked.

Jenny quickly tried to change the subject.

"I believe the Germans had a hospital here during the war?" she said.

"I wouldn't be going to that place," snapped Maud. "I had enough of the Germans during the war when I was a young girl, I certainly do not want to be reminded of that time again."

Jenny put her empty cup on the table and told Maud they would have to go as she had some shopping to do. She promised to pick up some fruit and vegetables for her and to drop them off the next day.

Once in the car, Jenny again mentioned that Maud was full of old stories which got muddled up in her mind, she went onto explain that old people often mix up fantasy with reality.

Ella remained quiet as she was secretly tingling inside as Maud had mentioned the old man and old woman. She thought to herself, *Could this be the old couple she had seen?* This was definitely intriguing.

The following Monday, Alison, James's mum, collected Ella and with both the boys headed off for a day at Gorey Castle. All three children were very excited; it wasn't every day you got to explore a castle by yourself.

Alison raced through the country lanes and in no time, they came upon a beautiful harbour village. Tiny sailing boats bobbed about in the water and a row of higgledy-piggledy white houses surrounded the cove. Rising majestically above them all was the mighty castle. It had grand views looking straight out over the sea.

Alison drove up the winding road to the entrance of the castle where they were met by a row of tourists all queuing to get in.

"Now," said Alison, "I am going to leave you children here. Check your watch, James; I make it almost twenty past ten. I will come back for you at twelve and we can find somewhere to eat, okay? Then if you want to explore some more, I will arrange to catch up with you all later."

James checked his watch and agreed that they would all meet back in the car park at midday.

"Take care," she reminded them. They all agreed and hastily got out of the car to join the line at the entrance to the castle.

"Great," said Marcus. "We have at least two hours to explore."

"The thing is where to first?" said James.

Marcus delved into his pocket and pulled out an old guidebook of Gorey Castle that his dad had given him.

"This may help," he replied.

The children poured over the pages whilst they were queuing. "Wow, there's the creature Maud told me about," said Ella, pointing to a picture of some sort of beast, which resembled a dragon, but there again it could have been some kind of pterodactyl.

"We'll certainly be taking a look at that," stated James. "Remember the verse?" he added. "That thing could be the mythical being."

Ella and Marcus stared in amazement. They hadn't thought of that but suddenly realised he could be absolutely right.

Have you ever been able to explore something by yourself? If you were James, Marcus or Ella where would you start to explore?
What do you think the children will find?

Chapter 11

The children made their way into the castle following a group of tourists. They entered a dark narrow passageway and following it through it opened out into a large room. On the wall at the far side hung a portrait of Queen Elizabeth II of England and on the opposite wall another portrait of Queen Elizabeth only this one was Queen Elizabeth I with a man painted into the picture. A group of tourists stood around this picture and a guide was telling them all it was a picture of Sir Walter Raleigh, a long-time favourite of Queen Elizabeth I, who was the Governor of Jersey from 1600 to 1603.

Ella looked around, the walls were made of heavy stone bricks and there was a huge open fireplace. Windows let in light but hundreds of years ago when the castle was first built, there would not have been any glass in them. A guide started again to talk about the room they were in and then to name some of the castles occupants.

The children looked at each other.

"I think it's time to do some exploring," whispered James.

He led the way out through a door on the other side of the room, Marcus and Ella followed close behind. They made their way through stone corridors and up a narrow stone staircase, turning left at the top they found themselves entering a dark passageway. It led them to a room at the end.

An amazing sight met their eyes as suspended from the ceiling was an incredible creature. It really did look as if it had just flown through the opening high up in the stonewall. The creature's head and neck were a golden colour and covered with leaf shaped scales that glinted in the light. The one large yellow eye they could see seemed to peer right at them and its huge beak was curved and open ready to snap up anything it fancied whilst four large sets of talons attached to each limb hung open, ready to grasp its prey.

"Gosh, he is scary," said Ella. "I wouldn't want to meet him on a dark night."

James pulled a piece of paper out of his pocket. He had written the poem they had found at the tower on it and he read it out:

> *Treasure lies deep within the Isle,*
> *To find it will be a trial,*
> *Seek the castle by Gorey Bay,*
> *And find the Gargoyle who knows the way.*
> *A mythical being rests inside this place.*
> *A creature you have no need to face,*
> *He guards something you will need,*
> *Seek the alcove to proceed.*

"Well, we're are at Gorey Castle and I think this is the mythical beast, we certainly have no need to face him as he looks pretty dead to me," said Marcus.

"So, it says he guards something we need," said James, "but what?"

"An alcove, that is what we have to find," added Marcus.

The children stepped further inside the room, which was dimly lit as the only light was coming from the window high up near the ceiling. They scanned the walls but could see nothing that resembled an alcove. Then Marcus glanced behind the big oak door, which was pushed back against the wall.

"I think there is something here," he gasped.

Carefully, the children pushed the heavy door away from the wall and sure enough, there was a small arch shaped alcove halfway up the wall. The children were not able to reach it, as it was too high up. James had an idea, he asked Marcus to cup his hands together to form a step so that he could get a bunk up with his foot. Marcus readily supported James as he hoisted himself up. His fingers could just about reach the ledge of the alcove.

"Lift me higher," yelled James. Marcus took a deep breath and slowly managed to raise his arms a little higher. James stretched with all his might and managed to get his hand in the alcove.

"There is something here," he shouted.

Suddenly, Marcus's arms gave way and the two boys tumbled to the ground. Both boys fell hard onto the stone floor. Ella let out a yell.

"Are you alright," she said.

They got to their feet and dusted themselves off.

"I think so, nothing broken," said Marcus shakily.

"What happened?" asked James.

"I am sorry," said Marcus. "I sort of lost my balance."

"Are you okay to try again?" James sighed.

"Are you crazy, of course we try again," answered Marcus.

"Do be careful," warned Ella. She was frightened that if they fell again, they would really hurt themselves.

"Okay, steady now," said Marcus and he bent down with his hands cupped together. "Just try and be quick," he added.

James stepped up and soon found the ledge. This time he managed to feel his way along the ledge of the alcove, his fingers felt something cold and hard. He was just about to grab it when he leant too far and over balanced. As he fell, his hand swiped along the bottom of the alcove and something flew out landing with a clang on the ground. Ella quickly picked it up.

Thankfully, James landed on his two feet. The boys quickly went to see what had fallen. Ella showed them. It was a thin metal rod, about three inches long, that had a loop at one end and was flattened at the other.

"What in heaven's name is that?" said Marcus quite disgusted seeing that it was really nothing.

"I don't know," said James intrigued. "It could be a key. It must be used for something."

Just then they heard footsteps and the children realised they needed to go. James slipped the strange metal object into the pocket of his shorts.

As they left the room, a young man and woman came in. They were delighted to see the mythical beast and started to take photos with their phones.

The children made their way back along the corridors and going through an open archway found themselves outside on a large balcony area looking out over the sea. The view was spectacular, the sun shone and the gentle breeze tossed the little boats about in the harbour below.

"You can see France if you look carefully," said Marcus.

The children took in the view and then turned to look at the castle itself, which stood directly behind them. According to the guidebook, the castle had once been a prison and Ella could imagine that it must have been a very daunting place despite the wonderful view.

Marcus looked at the castle turrets.

"I don't see any gargoyles on the tops of the walls, do you?"

"Actually," answered James, "you're right, but there must be at least one gargoyle here somewhere as the poem says it knows the way, maybe they are on the other side."

The children headed off along a covered pathway and into a courtyard where they passed a statue of a knight on horseback, which was life size and looked incredibly real. He was carrying a lamb and his horse looked as if it wanted to talk to you as its head was inclined to one side.

The children headed towards another set of stone stairs, passing a wooden plinth that held three metal figures, depicting prisoners, chained to it.

"So, there was a prison here," said Marcus.

"They obviously were not treated well judging by the figures there," added James.

Ella thought how sad they looked and what a cold reminder it was of the past.

The children hurried on making their way to the castle turrets. Here they found a room that had a large wooden disc on the wall. This disc had twenty tiny bottles around the outside all containing coloured liquid and some ancient writing on it. There was a man in the room that was dressed in a medieval costume and he welcomed them telling them to come and take a closer look.

"What on earth is this?" asked Marcus.

The man dressed in the medieval costume told them it was a Urine Wheel. He went onto say that way back in the medieval times, doctors used people's urine to find out what was wrong with them.

"How could they do that?" asked Ella.

"Well," said the man, "they would taste it, for instance if it was very sweet then the likelihood was that the patient might have diabetes."

"Taste it!" exclaimed Marcus. "That is really disgusting."

"Observing the colour of urine or tasting it long ago was the only way to find out what was wrong with them," said the man.

Just then, James's phone rang; it was his mother. He answered it saying he was sorry and they would come right away.

"It's quarter past twelve and Mum is in the car park waiting for us," he gasped.

The man dressed in the medieval clothes gave them directions to the exit and the children scampered off. The time had flown by. They certainly needed to come back after their lunch as they had not found the gargoyle if indeed there was one to find.

What do you think the metal rod the children have found could be?
What would you have enjoyed seeing at the castle?
How would you feel having to taste urine?

Chapter 12

Half an hour later, the children were sitting in the Gorey Crab Shack enjoying crab sandwiches for lunch. Ella had never eaten crab before and was not at all sure she would like it. When she bit into the bread, she couldn't believe the taste, the pink and white flesh was sweet yet slightly salty and the meat itself soft with a rich taste of its own.

"Is it good?" asked Alison.

"No," replied Ella, "it's delicious."

They all laughed. The boys of course had tasted crab many times and were tucking in hungrily.

Alison asked them all what they had seen that morning. Obviously, they did not mention they had found the metal rod but told her of the creature and the statues and of course the Urine Wheel. They also said they would like to go back that afternoon.

Once lunch was over, Alison took them back to the castle and told them that Ella's Aunt Lucy would pick them up at 4 p.m. She made James check his watch. It was now five past two.

"Please do not be late and leave Ella's aunt waiting," she said firmly.

The children promised to be on time.

As soon as Alison had gone, the children went back into the castle showing their tickets.

"Now," said James, "we have to find a gargoyle."

"What if it's on top of the wall," said Ella.

Marcus looked at James. "No matter where it is, we find it. Right," he said.

"Right," said James.

The children walked around the courtyard for the next twenty minutes looking up at the walls but could not find anything that resembled a gargoyle. They then followed some steps that took them through archways and up to a long, narrow corridor. Here they ventured into a room off to the right. In a dark corner was a huge statue of a medieval soldier that had arrows, spears and knives sticking out from his body. It was showing all the different ways in which a man could die in battle and the terrible wounds that he could receive from the enemy.

"Not a pretty sight," said Marcus.

"I wouldn't have wanted to be a knight in those days," added James as he stared at the sword that was poking out of the knight's eye.

"Can we move on," said Ella who was not the least bit impressed by the spectacle.

Once again, they travelled along more gloomy corridors that seemed to go off in every direction and soon stumbled across another room that housed a metal tree with lots of heads on it. The children read the plaque that stood by the side of it. They discovered that it was called The Tree of Succession and showed the Medieval French and English Kings and Queens. Three statues stood as the bark and the leaves were all the heads. The faces seemed very lifelike; they were serious and quite macabre as they stared out at the visitors.

"This place is really creepy," said Ella.

"Not the sort of place to be spending a lot of time in," added Marcus.

"I think all castles are the same," said James. "I certainly wouldn't like to live in one, they're cold and more like prisons than places to live. Come on, we have to concentrate on trying to find this gargoyle?"

The children left the chamber and made their way back along yet more corridors and down more stone steps until they found themselves in a courtyard that overlooked the village of Gorey.

"Well, it must be nearly time to meet Aunt Lucy," said Ella.

James quickly looked at his watch. "It's only twenty past three," said James. "We have plenty of time."

The children looked around and Ella went over to the low wall to take in a better view of the harbour. She looked out across the sparkling ocean that stretched out to the horizon. Suddenly she gasped, as there below, staring up at her, was the old man with his gold spectacles and old woman with her cloche hat on. She called the boys, and hearing the urgency in her voice, they came running over to her. They stared back at the very odd couple who turned and slowly walked away.

"Come on," said James. "We have to catch them."

The children ran down an old brick stairwell leaping over the steps two by two. As soon as they reached the bottom, they headed right in the direction they had seen the old people. They found themselves at ground level near the exit where there was a narrow gateway. As they stared through, they saw the odd couple who turned to face them and then in a blink of an eye, they seemed to disappear and the only things remaining were two magpies that fluttered and squawked in their place.

"Magpies," said Ella under her breath. "Two for joy."

"What do you mean, Ella," enquired James.

"It's the old rhyme," said Ella. "Do you not know it? One for sorrow, two for joy, three for a girl, four for a boy, five for silver, six for gold, seven for a secret never to be told. It's two for joy."

"I have never heard of that," said Marcus dismissively.

"I am sure they were the old people Maud saw and she said she wondered what they wanted, I am sure they are telling us something," said Ella.

They watched the birds flutter around and they went towards the gateway. They fluttered and squawked around the gatepost. James suddenly shouted, "Look there on the gate post."

The children stared at the old gatepost, which seemed to be crumbling with age and there at the top of one of the posts sat a funny little stone creature.

"It's a gargoyle," said James.

The children rushed over to get a closer look.

The magpies continued to fly around the gargoyle and one of them started to peck at the back of its fat neck. They then flew off onto the lawn close by.

Ella went round the other side to view the back of the gatepost. It stood about four feet high. The ugly little creature sat on the top. She scrutinised the little statue. It stood about a foot tall and was naturally made of stone, which was quite worn and disintegrating with age. Its face was quite ugly with its wide mouth open in a peculiar grin and its little hands were clasped together in front of him. The eyes were bulbous and seemed to be staring out at them even though they were made of stone. It was in a crouched position.

"Take a look at this," said Ella to the boys.

She pointed to a darkened area at the back of the gargoyle's neck, there appeared to be a crevice where the neck joined the body.

"I wonder," said James. "Can this have anything to do with this gargoyle?"

He produced the funny looking rod thing they had found and held it up by the loop at the end.

Marcus picked up a stick from the ground and started to scrap around the back of the neck. Fine dust from the stone flew out and the crevice became more visible. James tentatively pushed the metal rod with the flat end into the dark opening and much to everyone's amazement it disappeared easily, leaving only the loop at the end. James tried to turn the loop clockwise, but it was not moving. Using both hands, he pressed even harder.

"Wait a minute," said Marcus and went over to the wall where he found a strong stick that he fed through the loop and using it as a lever, the boys were able to push the metal loop clockwise, slowly it began to move. There was a scrapping sound and the gargoyle began to shift to the right, ever so slightly.

"Come on," said James. "A little bit more."

The boys made a huge effort and the statue slid a few more centimetres leaving a small opening in the gatepost below. Marcus cautiously slid his two fingers into the gap and was able to feel something. He pinched his two fingers together around what seemed like a piece of material but was in fact a small pouch and he cautiously pulled it out through the opening. Once removed, James turned the loop anti clockwise using the lever and with a rasping scrape, the statue fell back into position.

"What are you up to," shouted a harsh voice from behind the children.

They instantly froze.

"I'm talking to you children," said an angry voice.

"Oh, God," said James under his breath, as they turned to face an older man.

"What is the problem," said James.

"I saw you move that stone statue," he said.

Marcus concealed the material pouch behind his back and sidled up to Ella so he could pass it to her.

At that point, a security guard came over. "What's the problem here," he said.

"These children were stealing that statue; I saw them move it."

The guard looked in amazement.

"I don't think so, sir," he replied. "That statue has been there for 800 years. These children would not be able to carry it."

"I am telling you," said the man. "These children were vandalising the statue and I saw them take something."

"Oh, really," said the guard in astonishment. "Well, let's see what they have done."

"We haven't done anything," said Marcus.

The guard checked the statue. "There is nothing wrong with the statue, it seems pretty solid to me," he added trying to move it.

The man looked at Ella. "You there," he said pointing to Ella, "you have got something behind your back."

Ella produced the bag,

"Yes," she said. "It's my purse."

She carefully wrapped her fingers around the material pouch hiding it from full view.

The man narrowed his eyes and looked them up and down.

"Oh, come on, George," said a lady. "Leave the children alone, they were only looking at the statue."

"They were vandalising it; I tell you," went on the man.

The woman turned to the children, and in a whisper said,

"I am sorry, he has not been well."

She turned to the man and the children heard her say, "Come on, let's go and have a nice cup of tea."

The security guard asked the children what they were doing now and James told him they were leaving as someone was collecting them at four.

"You better get a move on," said the guard. "It's nearly ten past now."

The children set off at a run for the exit. Ella gripped tightly the bag as they fled and the magpies flew away chirping to each other.

Why do you think the man accused the children of vandalising the Gargoyle?
How would you have felt if you had been caught doing something that you shouldn't really be doing?
Do you think the old man and woman are there to help the children?
What do you think will be in the pouch?

Chapter 13

Aunt Lucy was in the car park waiting.

"Ah! There you all are," she said smiling. "I was beginning to get worried."

The children piled into the back of the Range Rover and Aunt Lucy sped off heading for St Martin's to take the boys back home first. Ella kept tight hold of the little pouch, which was made of rough linen and was quite dirty with age. She could feel something inside but did not dare to look for fear her Aunt Lucy would notice.

Aunt Lucy kept asking them questions about their trip to the castle as she navigated the country lanes. The boys sat impatiently wanting to examine the pouch, but they knew they daren't at that moment. The drive seemed to take forever before they reached the outskirts of the town. Within minutes, Aunt Lucy pulled up outside James's house and Alison appeared smiling welcoming them all back.

Ella knew instantly there would be no time to examine the content of the pouch today so thinking quickly on her feet she asked Aunt Lucy if the boys could come over to have lunch with them tomorrow and see the potato farm. Of course, the boys appeared to be very enthusiastic about this, well James did anyway.

Aunt Lucy said that would be fine and that after lunch they could all maybe help with the potato picking.

James said that would be great. He shot Marcus a look that said he better agree too.

Marcus wasn't at all happy; digging in the earth for potatoes certainly wasn't his idea of fun. He did however see the look James gave him and hastily agreed.

Arrangements were made for the following day and Ella and Aunt Lucy left for Spud End. Ella concealing the precious pouch, managed to slide it into her pocket for safekeeping.

It wasn't until late that evening when Ella was ready for bed that she had a chance to look closely at the pouch. It was tightly closed at the top by a black cord. Ella carefully prised it open and inside was a piece of paper folded in four. Ella removed it and leaving the bag on the bed took the paper over to the bedside lamp so she could get a better look at it. As she bent over towards the light, the door opened and Aunt Lucy suddenly burst into the room, carrying some clean clothes of Ella's that she had just ironed. Ella quick as a flash dropped the paper onto the floor then stood up and with her foot pushed the paper under the bed. Her Aunt placed the clothes down on the blue bed cover and straight away noticed the small pouch lying there.

"Where did you get this?" she asked picking it up. Ella told her she had found it at the castle.

"It's got a swastika on it, look. Do you know what this is, Ella?"

Ella had not noticed the black symbol on the bag at all.

"No," she said.

"Well, it's a swastika, a symbol of the German Nazi Party that controlled this island during the war. In fact, I think it is the Nazi German Flag, but the red around it has faded away. It is obviously very old. I'd better keep this, as it is not a nice thing for you to have. Where did you say you found it?"

Ella went very red but managed to answer that Marcus had found it by the gatepost at the castle and had given it to her. Aunt Lucy took the pouch and after tucking her up in bed, said goodnight and went downstairs.

As soon as she heard her aunt descend the stairs, Ella jumped out of bed and quickly retrieved the paper from the floor. She carefully began to open it out fully. The paper was so brittle with age that it began to crumble. There was some writing on it, but it was in that old script that was very difficult to read. Ella got her notepad and decided that she would write down the text as best as she could.

By the dim light of the bedside lamp, Ella copied down the words meticulously. She tried to read it all once she had finished, but it made no sense to her. *Better to wait for the boys tomorrow,* she thought. Ella decided to put the clue under Horace's jacket. She gently folded the crumbling parchment and slipped it neatly out of sight.

Horace was her stuffed furry rabbit that had a cute tweed jacket, which made him look quite old. He was sat on her bed and took pride of place on the corner of her pillow each night. He had been with Ella as long as she could remember and she was very fond of him. He knew all her secrets as she told him everything even though he could never answer her. She knew it would be safe there and the notepad she put under her pillow until the morning.

What would you have done if you had been Ella?
Would you have told your Aunt all about the Gargoyle?
Why do you think Aunt Lucy didn't want Ella to have the pouch?

Chapter 14

The next day couldn't come soon enough for Ella; the boys arrived mid-morning this time with Marcus's dad Tom. He introduced himself and was pleased to join Aunt Lucy in the kitchen for a cup of coffee. After a refreshing glass of lemonade each, the three friends followed Aunt Lucy's advice and went out for a walk to work up an appetite for lunch.

Ella retraced her steps from her first day and led the boys through the forest, which was teeming with life as usual, but they did not have time to enjoy the animal or plant life. As they hurried along, Ella told the boys of what had happened the night before with Aunt Lucy.

"A Swastika," yelled James. "Wow, we are definitely onto something."

"What do you mean," said Marcus. "There are a lot of old Second World War mementoes in that old antique place in Baroque Square in St Helier. My mum is in there all the time, looking, she says for something interesting. What I want to know is what was in the pouch?"

They stopped under the shade of the tall forest trees and Ella produced the paper she had made the notes on and read its contents:

The island's treasure is hidden well
In a spot that is a living hell
Go North West to find the hoard
Follow the winding path toward
A vast cavern where the sea wildly churns
Amidst tall trees and the dark green ferns
Beelzebub will be waiting for you
Find him, as he has the very last clue.

"Gosh," said James, "this is going to take some thinking about."

"What or who is a Bel…zel…bub?" said Ella.

"Not a Scooby," said Marcus, "but we will have to find out as he has a clue for us."

Ella gave the paper to James who slipped it into his pocket for safekeeping. The children walked on deep in thought until the path gave way to the beautiful lavender field.

"What is that pong?" cried Marcus.

"It's lavender; do you not like the smell?" said Ella.

"Obviously not," said James.

"The stones are the other side of this field," said Ella.

The children followed a narrow path that skirted the edge of the field until they came to the country lane. Carefully, they shot across the roadway and dived into the hedgerow venturing into the leafy tunnel. It soon opened out and there before them were the stones.

"Oh, yes," said Marcus. "This is a Dolmen. I have been to others just like it, with my dad."

"Is it a burial ground?" enquired Ella.

"Absolutely, in fact it was probably made around 2000 BC. My dad would love to take a look at this."

"Sh! be quiet," said James.

They all stood very still. There was a rustling noise as the leaves on the shrubs and trees began to shake. The gentle breeze that had been blowing got stronger and a few droplets of water fell, the sky darkened as a large black cloud moved in front of the sun.

"Here comes the rain," shouted James and the children ran for cover under the only place they could see, which was the huge stone that lay across the end of the passageway of smaller stones. They crouched beneath as large rain drops began to pelt down. They huddled together watching and listening. The shower at first was quite loud as it washed over the greenery and hit the stones with a slapping sound, but then it seemed to ease and the sound became softer and the constant pit pat turned to a light tap as the rain drops eventually ceased. It seemed to be getting brighter. As they watched birds started to descend onto the shrubs and grass, ready to pluck the newly washed grubs that lay on the leaves. Slowly, they emerged from their shelter and as they did, they were met with a wonderful fresh smell, everything was clean and newly washed, the greenery looking somehow much brighter.

There over by the entrance stood a beautiful young woman with long wavy, honey coloured hair. She stretched up and pulled a flower from the hedgerow and smelled its sweet fragrance closing her eyes as she breathed in the scent. Although she did not appear to have an umbrella, she was not the least bit wet. Her hair was loose and her long flowing yellowy green dress completely dry. She turned to look at the children and smiled. The children stood motionless watching her, as she appeared to fade away, disappearing with a rustle into the hedgerow.

"Who are these people that just disappear," said Marcus.

I have seen her somewhere before, I am sure, said Ella deep in thought.

"How come she wasn't wet, where did she shelter from that heavy shower?" asked James.

The other two could not say, as there did not appear to be any other shelter, but the one they had been in.

Ella realised then who the lady looked like; she was the image of the figures on the panels in the glass church. She decided not to mention that to the boys.

James suggested they went back to the farm for lunch. They were all very quiet on the return journey not really knowing what to make of it all. They agreed that they would find out whatever they could about the verse they had found and meet later in the week to see what they should do next. Baffled by what had happened, they needed time to take it all in.

What do you make of it all?
Have you ever been caught in a heavy shower?
Do you remember the smell the rain leaves?
If you were Ella, what would you do next?

Chapter 15

A few days later, Ella went for another visit with Jenny to see Maud. She had not been well and Jenny was quite worried about her. This time, Jenny made the tea for them all while Maud sat in her comfy chair with a shawl wrapped around her shoulders. She had caught a bit of a chill from being out in the garden one evening too long when the air had become quite damp.

Ella sat on the sofa and told her all about her visit to Gorey Castle with the boys. She did not want to say anything about the gargoyle or the clue they had found but was interested to know if Maud knew who 'Bayzelbub' was. Jenny was busy in the kitchen and well out of earshot so Ella asked Maud if there was anyone on the island with that name.

Maud was silent for a bit and then said she had never heard of anyone by that name living on Jersey. Ella then asked her quietly if she knew where there might be a cavern or cave near the sea or anywhere where the water rushed in. Maud sat back in her chair and for a few minutes was very quiet. Ella thought that perhaps she was going to fall asleep, but suddenly, she lifted her head and her eyes were sparkling.

"There are lots of caves along the rugged coast line of the island, but I think you may mean Devil's Hole," she said. "There is an old collapsed cave there and the seawater flows right into it. It's a big tourist attraction so I have heard," she added. She then began to chuckle.

"Did you say Bayzelbub?" Ella nodded. "I think you meant to say 'Beelzebub', it is a name given to the devil."

Ella suddenly felt a tingling sensation when she heard this, but just at that moment, Jenny breezed in with tea and three custard tarts for them.

"Here you are," she announced. "This will perk you up, Maud," she said and handed Maud a steaming cup of tea.

"So, what have you two been chatting about?" she asked.

"Maud was just telling me about Devil's Hole," said Ella timidly.

"Oh! That is worth seeing, Ella," said Jenny. "A very interesting place, it was one of the first sights Art took me to. We walked up and looked down to see this enormous hole in the cave where the sea comes rushing in and out swirling around. There are the most spectacular views of the sea and rugged coastline all around too, and would you believe that someone years ago actually carved a statue in wood of the devil. There is still a statue there today. It is the size of a grown man. I suppose that is why it is called Devil's Hole." Jenny stopped to take a bite of her custard tart.

Ella felt a bit better after hearing Jenny's description; suddenly it didn't seem that bad a place.

"So it's a tourist attraction, is it?" asked Ella.

"Oh, yes," replied Jenny, "it is very popular too."

Maud than told them she had visited the place many times, but the last time was several years ago.

"So why is it a devil statue?" asked Ella.

"Well," said Maud, "so the story goes a long, long time ago a figure head from an old sailing vessel was washed up in the hole possibly from a shipwreck. Someone found it and fished it out of the hole; they then carved it into the devil statue, adding horns and other bits to it, obviously over time it got a bit worse for wear as it was made of wood."

"The statue is now made out of metal and stands in a pool of water so visitors can see him as they go on the trail down to the actual hole," added Jenny as she sipped her tea. "Art told me that the hole in the rock was made hundreds of years ago when a cave collapsed."

"But why make it a devil?" asked Ella.

Ella was a little superstitious and did not like anything that might be bad or that might be associated with the devil or black magic. She certainly did not want to be associated with anything of that kind.

"Oh, it's just a bit of fun," said Jenny. "It must have been quite a dangerous place years ago so I would think to deter people from going there they made out it was a bit spooky. As the sea rushes in and out, it does make eerie noises, which are enough to frighten anyone. You have to visit; it would be fun."

Maud looked at Ella. "You called it a different name," she said.

"Oh!" said Ella, thinking fast, "I heard James say Bayzelbub."

"Beelzebub," said Maud in a whisper. "He has many names that one, Satin, Old Nick, Diablo, they all mean the same thing, The Devil."

Ella finished her tea and put down her cup. *Well, one thing was for sure*, she thought to herself, *like it or not she was going to have to go to see this statue and get whatever it is from it.*

On the way back to Spud End, Jenny remarked that she was sure Art would like to go to Devil's Hole again and maybe they could arrange a trip to take her. Ella mentioned that she thought perhaps the boys would like to go too. Jenny said she would see what Art wanted to do and would let her know.

That evening, Jenny and Art joined Ella, Aunt Lucy and Uncle Josh for supper at Spud End. Aunt Lucy had cooked a whole salmon and served it with a delicious crab sauce, new potatoes [from the farm] and a large bowl of salad. The fish was simply mouth-watering. Ella normally didn't like fish, but since she came to stay at Spud End, she had developed a definite taste for the fish her aunt served, which was always baked or steamed with a delectable sauce to accompany it.

As they were all tucking in with enjoyment, Jenny spoke to Art about Devil's Hole. She said she thought they should take Ella along with her friends. Art was pleased to agree and it was arranged for the following Sunday. He also said if they went in the afternoon, they could go to The Priory Inn, which was in St Mary's nearby for lunch. It was left with Aunt Lucy to arrange it with James's mum Alison.

Uncle Josh was a bit concerned about the trip they were arranging as he had never been and had heard that the walk there could be hazardous as it went by very steep cliffs. Jenny reassured him that it would not be a problem as long as they kept to the path; there really was no danger.

Ella sat and wondered how they were going to get near to the Devil's statue to get the clue when she remembered that Jenny had told her that the statue was in a pool of water. That must be away from the pathway for sure. The message did say it was the Devil that would give them the last clue. She kept tight-lipped and thought she would speak to the boys about it all as she was positive, they would be able to find a way to get close to Beelzebub.

That evening, Ella called James and mentioned about the trip. He had been speaking with Marcus and they had both worked it out that Devil's Hole was where they needed to go once they had discovered who Beelzebub was. He thanked Ella for arranging it all. She explained it wasn't down to her actually as Maud was the one that had thought about it and Jenny the one that wanted to take her to Devil's Hole. Ella explained it could be difficult getting near to the statue. James told her not to worry as he and Marcus would certainly find a way. Ella was unsure about it all but thought it would be best to leave it all up to the boys.

Are you superstitious?
Were you aware the Devil had so many different names?
Do you know of any others?
Would you be a bit unnerved going to something like the Devil's Hole?

Chapter 16

Much to the children's annoyance, it was decided that everyone, including the parents, would meet at The Priory Inn for lunch. Art and Jenny had agreed to walk the path to Devil's Hole and the parents could follow on later if they wished. The boys were not at all happy about this scenario as they certainly did not want their parents there but arrangements were made so there was no choice but to accept them.

When Ella arrived, James was there with his parents Alison and Greg who greeted them warmly. Aunt Lucy then introduced Uncle Josh, Art and Jenny. Twenty minutes later, Marcus arrived with his parents Penny and Tom. Thankfully, Greg had booked a table as the small inn was not used to such big parties for lunch and of course, this time of year was very busy. The children sat at a table by themselves and left the adults to their own conversation.

"Let's look at that clue again," said Marcus.

James had written it out on a piece of paper and they all surveyed it. "We're certainly in the right place," said Marcus. "We just need to get near to that statue."

"What's that?" said the familiar voice of Tom, Marcus's dad.

James thought quickly. "Oh! this, it's just a game we are playing, I have written some clues to see if they can guess where it is I am thinking of."

Tom looked puzzled but decided not to ask any further questions and simply requested what they wanted from the menu.

The children ordered and then sat quietly until their food arrived.

"Why did our parents have to come," said James.

"Don't worry," said Marcus. "We know we have to find something at the Devil's statue and I think we can lose them for five minutes while we investigate."

"Let's hope so," said James.

As soon as lunch was finished, the adults were deep in conversation, laughing and joking. The children were keen to get underway to see this amazing cave. James took it upon himself to ask them when they could get started. Art was happy to get going and told the children to follow him. Jenny also decided to go with them and she and the children followed Art who led them to a steep pathway behind The Priory Inn, which led down the cliff face.

The pathway was not that easy to walk along as it was made of large and small stones in parts or loose gravel that crunched under their feet. It took them through partial woodland, which was very green and in parts, over grown. The sunlight shone through the foliage and speckled their way along the path. They walked at a steady pace listening to the sounds of birds tweeting in the trees, which provided a canopy over their heads. It was cool as a gentle breeze softly blew and the odd flies and flying insects darted around them flitting from one plant to the other. Ella noticed that the right side of the pathway was fenced off with a wooden framed fence of wire about four feet high. Greenery grew through it so it looked all part of the landscape.

Marcus suddenly spied something through the shrubbery. It looked at first like a man, but then he could see it was not moving and that there were two prongs coming out of its forehead. He nudged the others and tilted his head to the right to point it out without drawing the adult's attention. Looking through the leaves, they could see a large, slightly bowed head. Curly horns protruded from the top of the head and large coiled ears, a bit like a donkey's, jutted out on either side of its skull. A few minutes later, Art stopped and pointed out the Devil statue as he stood amidst a shaded clearing in the woodland area.

From where Art stood, they could see the whole thing. The children noticed he did not have any hands, but nonetheless, he looked extremely scary. His face held an arrogant expression, with a nasty sneer imprinted on it. Deep lines on his cheeks made him look old and his head had groves, which resembled wavy hair, which seemed to run across his head. He stood looking very powerful with strong muscles carved into his chest and arms. His lower body, from his waist to his knees, was made to look hairy and his feet were cloven making him look half man and half beast.

"Wow! He's massive," exclaimed Marcus.

Art laughed. "Well, I believe he is at least ten feet tall; you certainly wouldn't want to meet him on a dark night."

The children stared. Ella knew what they were all thinking. How on earth were they going to get anywhere near this statue and where for heaven's sake was he concealing a clue.

They moved on their way down the path and in front of them on the left-hand side was a little shelter with a thatched roof. Standing inside were two people watching as they passed. Ella glanced sideways and immediately her heart skipped a beat, as there were the two old people who she had seen several times before. They smiled at her and the old man took off his hat and nodded a greeting. Ella carried on walking, her heart thumping in her chest. The boys hadn't noticed them and Ella was reluctant to tell them in case Art and Jenny heard. She walked on keeping close to the boys.

The pathway continued through the hedgerows and passed the side of a house. It was then that Ella noticed the two magpies. They seemed to be flying over them and cawing loudly. Ella got the strangest feeling that the birds were trying to tell them something. They then flew behind them back up to where the statue stood, continuing their cawing as if trying to tell them to follow. In a matter of seconds, five other magpies joined the other two and they flapped and squawked noisily.

"What a lot of magpies," said Jenny turning around.

"Seven for a secret never to be told," said Ella softly.

"What was that?" said Jenny.

"I just said there are seven birds altogether," said Ella hastily.

"Oh, as many as that, I don't think I have ever seen that before," she said. "Come on, follow Art or you'll get left behind." With that, she walked swiftly on to catch up with her husband.

James signalled to Marcus who raced back up the path scattering the magpies as he went.

James grabbed Ella's arm.

"Come on," he said. "Let Marcus do what he needs to do."

Ella was about to protest but realised that Marcus and James had obviously arranged all this beforehand. She briskly walked on with James catching up with Jenny and Art.

"I wouldn't want to live anywhere near here," exclaimed Ella who really was quite frightened especially after seeing the daunting figure of the Devil.

Jenny laughed. "It's just a statue, Ella," she said reassuringly.

Within minutes, the path led them to a spectacular view of the sea. Its sudden blueness on the horizon made Ella feel less gloomy. To look out at the bay below with its rugged coastline and to see the waves running to shore with their tips of white surf just looked splendid on such a glorious sunny day as the one they were experiencing. They all stopped to admire the view and James came and stood beside Ella.

"What is Marcus doing?" she whispered nervously.

"Don't worry about him," whispered back James. "He'll find the clue come what may. He is old enough and ugly enough to look after himself," he added with a grin.

Marcus was as James had rightly said intent on finding the clue. He managed to climb over the wired fence, which bent dangerously under his weight. He fell with a thud on the other side and quickly picked himself up and hid behind a tree as he heard a group of people coming along the path. They stopped to admire the statue. Marcus waited breathing heavily and as soon as they moved on, he walked towards the statue. Within minutes, his right shoe filled with water and he found himself ankle deep in an algae covered pool.

Marcus crouched down to view the statue more closely and that is when he saw her. Just opposite in the trees was the beautiful lady they had seen at the Dolmens that rainy day. Her long golden hair hung loose and she wore a soft pale green yellow dress that appeared to camouflage her well. She looked across and beckoned him to join her. She moved further into the undergrowth. Marcus carefully waded behind the statue towards her. As he got close to her, she seemed almost transparent, her skin was clear and porcelain white, and her emerald green eyes sparkled. She smiled and then in a gentle kind voice, she told him she was glad he had come.

"Who are you?" he asked.

"That is not important," she exclaimed. "You seek the treasure, am I right?"

"Yes," replied Marcus. "We found the clues and hoped they were true."

"Oh, yes the treasure is very real," she said. "We can help you to find it."

"I have to get another clue from the statue, which is what the last clue said. Can you help me to do that?" Marcus hastily asked.

The lady looked at Marcus and smiled. I am afraid we tricked you she explained. We wanted to see if you really were brave enough and even interested enough to find the treasure. So, we got you to come here. Some people would have been too frightened to come this far. You have shown us that you are fearless and most certainly are able to find the hoard. The next step is not easy. It will take a lot of courage if you are to find the treasure. We can help you and we will guide you, so listen carefully.

She stretched up and took a little box down from the branch of a tree. The box was made of bark. She held it out to him in the palm of her hand and told Marcus the next clue was inside.

This clue you need to decipher, understand what it means and do your best to locate where the treasure lies. We will guide you if need be.

Marcus took the box. It was as light as a feather and looked very fragile.

"Thank you," he said taking the box from her. "Who are you?" he asked again.

"I have many names, Annabel, Diana, but you might have heard me called Titania. Your playwright named me that when he wrote A Midsummer Night's Dream," said the beautiful lady.

"You mean you are faerie?" gasped Marcus in total disbelief and astonishment.

"No, I am *not* a faerie, I am Queen of the Faeries," said the lady, who was obviously quite put out by being referred to as just a faerie.

"I am sorry," stuttered Marcus. "I didn't mean any disrespect."

"You had best watch your tongue, as here in the woodlands there are many faeries. You do not want to upset us. Faeries are normally kind and helpful, but do not dare to cross us, we have and can use magic powers. Do you understand?" she said glaring at Marcus. He nodded positively.

"We are able to change by a process of metamorphosis, so when we want you to see us, we can use human or animal form," she added.

Marcus thought of the old man and the old woman and the black dog. Were they faeries? He really wasn't sure about all this.

"Why are you helping us to find the treasure?" Marcus asked.

"As children you will follow what we say, as you have done so far. Of course, when you find the treasure you must pay us what it is worth."

"How are we going to do that?" asked Marcus.

"We faerie folk love nature, you humans destroy nature sometimes. You must help nature to thrive. We ask that you show humans how to look after the woodlands and the countryside on this island and protect nature for both yourselves and us," she said.

Marcus agreed but realised this was no easy task. "I will do my best," he said.

"Go find your friends and view the clue. Be brave, we will be with you." With that, she seemed to evaporate into thin air right before his eyes.

Marcus tucked the box into the pocket of his shorts and waded back to where he had to climb back over the fence and join his friends.

What do you make of all this?
If you were Marcus, do you think your friends would believe you had been speaking to a Faerie Queen?
Do you think looking after the countryside would be an easy job to reward the faeries?

Chapter 17

Marcus raced back along the path to catch up with the others.

It wasn't long before he spied Jenny coming towards him.

"Where have you been?" she asked anxiously.

"Oh, I needed to go to the loo," said Marcus quickly.

"You should have told me you wanted to go and we would all have waited for you. What on earth have you done to your trainers?" Jenny remarked.

Marcus looked down at his feet. In his excitement at obtaining the clue, he had totally forgotten that he had stepped in water. His socks were saturated and his once beautiful white trainers were now a blotchy green colour, as they were covered in horrid algae.

"Ah!" exclaimed Marcus. "Didn't notice that the ground was a bit wet."

Jenny was just about to say, what was his mother was going to think, when there came a shout from Art who was further along the path with Ella and James.

"Never mind now," Jenny said with a sigh. "Let's catch up with the others."

The pathway gave way to a platform across the cliffs and from there they could look down to Devil's Hole below. At first, all they could see far below was what appeared to be a large hole in the rock face. Then there came a tremendous gushing sound like fifty showers all being turned on full at once, the noise was quite deafening. Seawater rushed into the empty space, crashing against the rocks and swirling around before it quickly ebbed away. Seconds later, more water appeared and splashed over the rocks sending a spray of crystal-clear droplets into the air.

"Brilliant, isn't it?" exclaimed Art.

The children were mesmerised, being quite overwhelmed by the force of the water and the sounds and smells it generated.

At the side of the path, there was an information plaque, which told the history of the place. It mentioned the wreck of a French Cutter off the coast and how the figure head had washed ashore right into the Devil's Hole. A local man managed to fish it out and he then carved arms and legs to the figurehead and made it into a devil.

Whilst the others were busy reading it, James took Marcus aside and asked him if he had found anything. Marcus had decided that he was not going to tell James he had met a faery Queen, not just yet anyway, as he would just laugh himself silly so he nodded and told him he had found a box near the statue, which wasn't a lie really, he told himself. James was too delighted to ask any further details and they agreed to look at it later when they were alone.

It had only taken about twenty minutes to walk down the path to view the hole and as Art pointed out, they could continue along the pathway that headed back to The Priory Inn where they could all then enjoy a rest and a well-earned drink.

The way back was quite a steep climb although the pathway was a bit smoother. As it was now late in the afternoon, it was cooler and the children were eager to get back to view this new clue, so they kept up a steady pace. They reached the roadway in no time; however, they were all quite hot and sweaty. The adults were still sat around a table chatting away and they didn't appear to have missed them at all.

They of course wanted to hear all about the Devil's Hole and Penny, Marcus's mum, wanted to know what had happened to Marcus's trainers. He tried to explain as best he could, but as everyone was laughing so much, he gave up.

"I can just imagine him standing ankle deep in water as he is doing a pee," said his dad shaking his head. "You numpty."

His mother just shook her head. "I hope no one was around to see that." She sighed. "Honestly, he'll be the death of me; he's always up to something."

"He's a boy," said Uncle Josh with a grin and everyone laughed again.

The children sat by themselves on another table and Greg came to ask what they would like to drink. As soon as they were alone, James asked Marcus to show them the clue. Carefully, Marcus extracted it from his pocket. Squeezing the lid off the small box, he pulled out a folded piece of paper. "Where did you find it?" said Ella. "Was it by the statue?" She was intrigued, as she couldn't see how on earth the small box could have been hidden on the statue.

Marcus ignored her questions and started to open out the tightly folded package.

No sooner had he started than Ella plucked it from his hands and put it in her lap out of sight as she saw a lady coming with a tray of drinks and bowls of ice cream. Greg came over too and said he thought they deserved a little treat along with the drinks. They thanked him and were quick to scoop the fruity ice into their mouths. "Enjoy," he said and went back to join the adults.

"Phew, that was close," said James. "Well done, Ella, quick thinking."

Ella gave the partially folded paper back to Marcus and gently he continued unfolding it. There were in fact two pieces of paper. One was a thicker creamy coloured parchment. When it was unfolded, it revealed an insignia stamped at the very top of it. It was of an eagle with its wings spread wide and in its talons was a ring with the sign of a swastika inside it.

"There's the Swastika again, it's the sign of the Nazis," said James.

"What do you mean the Nazis? What have they got to do with treasure?" said Marcus quizzically.

"I don't know, but I am telling you this is an official piece of paper," replied James. "That is their insignia," he said.

Under the bold insignia was some writing, only the words didn't seem to make sense.

Zimmermann ist tot. Der Rest von uns muss morgen die Insel verlassen. Der Schatz ist gut versteckt. Nur vier von uns kennen jetzt den Standort. Wir werden zurückkommen und einen Weg finden, es zu bekommen.
Helmut Schatz

"That is German, I am sure," said Ella.

"That makes sense if it is to do with the Nazis," explained James.

"Never mind that, what do you make of this other piece of paper?" said Marcus.

The second sheet was on very thin paper almost like tissue and the writing was in a very fancy script just like the previous clues.

Find where the one of seven lies
An only girl, a beauty with haunting eyes
A flower of Jersey to be sure
An actress, socialite and so much more
Next to her, you will find the one
A soldier, who sleeps without his gun
He holds the key to the treasure you seek
Find him, search and don't be meek
For years the treasure was hidden away
By those that need no longer stay
Now's the time to find the hoard
Maybe also to collect a reward.

"What on earth does all that mean?" said Marcus.

"Heaven knows," said Ella, "but I think I know someone who can help us."

The boys looked at her.

"Maud," she said. "We have to talk to Maud."

Have you ever told little white lies when you don't want someone to know what you are doing?

Do you think Marcus was right not to mention the faeries to James?

Would you want to get an adult involved in solving the clue or would you want to keep it just between you and your friends?

Chapter 18

"We can't tell any grown up what we have found Ella," said James.

"Why not?" asked Ella. "Maud is perfect, she has lived on Jersey all her life so she is the best one to ask about the island and she believes there is treasure here."

"Yes, but she will tell other people what we are doing," added Marcus.

"Listen," said Ella, "Maud is nearly ninety-four years old and she is pretty switched on for her age; however, most people think she is gaga and just full of stories so if she does say anything no one is going to believe a word."

"You have a point there," said James. "How can we get to visit her?"

"Let me see if I can arrange it again with Jenny," said Ella.

"Can I come too?" asked Marcus. "I'd love to meet her."

"Me too," said James.

It was left with Ella to speak with Jenny and arrange a visit to see Maud. Jenny was delighted to hear that Ella would like to see Maud again and promised she would take her when she next went. When Ella asked if the boys could go too, Jenny was not too sure. She felt it maybe too much for Maud. Ella begged her to ask Maud as the boys really wanted to meet her.

The following Monday, Jenny spoke with Maud who was only too pleased to meet the children and agreed to them all coming the very next day.

In preparation, Ella had learnt the clue off by heart so she would be able to talk to Maud about it without having any papers. They had to be careful, as Jenny would be there too.

At two o'clock Tuesday afternoon, they all arrived at Maud's little terraced house. James had brought a cake from his father's bakery for Maud. She was at the door to welcome them all. After her cold Maud had made a good recovery, but she was still a bit weak and Jenny made her sit down whilst she went to make tea and cut the cake.

"I'm sure the children can keep you entertained whilst I am in the kitchen," she said.

Maud looked at James and asked him if his name was James Lamond. When he nodded positively, she chuckled to herself. She told James he looked very much like his great-grandfather. *James was puzzled, what on earth was she talking about, she must be rambling and thinking about something else,* he thought. Maud got up cautiously and shuffled over to a sideboard and pulled open a drawer. Sifting around, she suddenly announced 'There it is' and came back to her chair with an old school photograph. She pointed to a boy in the picture. "There's your great-grandfather and that's me, we were at school together." She smiled. "William Lamond, the baker's boy." She chuckled. Much to James' astonishment, the boy in the photograph did look a bit like him. Maud also told him she knew that it was his great-great-grandfather that had started the bakery. James was impressed; this woman was anything but gaga.

Whilst Jenny was away in the kitchen, Ella asked Maud if she knew of a Jersey flower. Maud sat back and closed her eyes, whispering softly, "Jersey flower. Do you mean the Battle of Flowers?"

"Oh, that's wonderful," said Jenny as she appeared with a pot of tea. "It's a carnival of flowers. It's an annual event here in St Helier and is on in August so you will see it providing you are still here, Ella." Jenny went back to the kitchen to get the cups and the cake.

James and Marcus rolled their eyes and glaring at each other, gave a sigh.

"No," said Marcus. "It is not that." Softly, he added, "We have a poem and it is about someone I think that was a Jersey flower, she may have been an actress."

Ella recited the first verse of the clue.

Suddenly, Maud's face creased into a broad smile. "You mean the Jersey Lily, that's who you're thinking of."

Jenny came into the room again and plonked a tray down with cups and saucers and a plate of sliced cake.

"Can you fetch the sugar and milk for me?" she asked James. "It's just on the side."

When James returned, Jenny proceeded to serve the tea.

Whilst they were tucking into the lovely sultana cake, Ella matter-of-factly asked Maud who this Jersey Lily was.

"Lillie Langtry, of course," she said. "Oh! She was a one really beautiful girl with dazzling eyes; she was an actress and caught the attention of The Prince of Wales and a lot of other noblemen too." Maud chuckled again.

"Is she still alive now?" asked Ella.

"Good grief, no," replied Maud. "She was born in Jersey and is buried here in the family tomb where her father was the rector. She was very spoilt as she had only six brothers no sisters, so she was the only girl and her parents over indulged her when she was a child." Maud tut-tutted shaking her head.

The children smiled, obviously Maud did not approve of spoilt children.

"Why are you talking about Lillie Langtry?" asked Jenny.

"I just heard about the Jersey Lily and wondered who or what it was," said Ella.

"Oh!" said Jenny. "She was quite notorious in her day, a real little socialite; she went to all the parties and grand openings and knew just about everybody that was anybody in those days. I don't know much else about her but do know she came from Jersey and is buried here in St Saviour's churchyard in St Helier; Art took me to see the tomb."

The children looked at each other. They now felt they understood the first half of the clue thanks to Maud and Jenny. *Find where the one of seven lies, an only girl, a beauty with haunting eyes. A flower of Jersey to be sure, an actress, socialite and so much more...*This was obviously Lillie Langtry and they knew they would have to go to the graveyard and find where she was buried to find who lay next to her, which according to the poem was a soldier.

The children agreed to meet up later in the week and try to understand the rest of the clue. In the meantime, it was decided to let Ella look after the clue as both James and Marcus had mums that went through their rooms. James had complained that his mum was forever tidying and throwing out anything she thought was rubbish, which was what had happened to the first clue. Marcus had said his mum did exactly the same whereas Ella was a guest and therefore her Aunt Lucy would not be throwing out anything that belonged to her. Ella took possession of the clue and had already decided that she would hide it along with the other clue in Horace's jacket.

The following Wednesday saw the children sitting on the beach by the tower studying the latest clue.

"Well, taking it that Lillie Langtry is the person the poem is talking about, we know she lies in St Saviour's churchyard in St Helier," said Marcus matter-of-factly.

"By the sounds of it, we have to look for someone whose grave is near hers. *Next to her you will find the one, a soldier who sleeps without his gun,*" said James.

"Well, soldiers aren't buried with their guns, are they?" questioned Ella.

"I wouldn't have thought so," said James.

"But if he is dead," said Marcus, "what can he tell us?"

"There may be something on his headstone," said Ella thoughtfully. "We won't know until we take a look."

It was agreed that they would go the following Friday to St Helier on the pretence of going to the cinema but would find the churchyard and seek out at least Lillie Langtry's tomb. Ella was not the least bit sure about this, as she didn't want to lie to Aunt Lucy and Uncle Josh. The boys told her it would be fine but even so, she had a bad feeling about it all.

Friday couldn't come soon enough for the three children. They had asked if they could go and watch the latest Jurassic Park movie, which was currently showing. Alison had agreed to drive them to St Helier and drop them outside the cinema for the afternoon viewing. As Uncle Josh had to come into St Helier later that afternoon, he agreed to collect them once the film was over.

Marcus got a map of St Helier and had planned out their route to St Saviour's church. It was a good thirty-minute walk from the cinema.

Thankfully, Friday was not a particularly warm day and when the children got to the cinema, they waved Alison goodbye then they headed along the road to join the high street. It was full of tourists and the children found themselves weaving in and out of people and buggies all meandering along viewing the shop windows in a leisurely fashion. They hurried along turning right and then up a steep road away from the town. They managed to keep up a brisk pace despite the fact that the route was mostly up hill.

Meanwhile back at Spud Farm, Aunt Lucy was in the middle of changing the bed sheets. She had just finished Ella's bed when she noticed Horace lying on the floor. She picked him up to put him on the pillow when her fingers felt something crackle beneath his little jacket. Aunt Lucy instinctively took a closer look, her curiosity getting the better of her, and removing the paper, she unfolded it to see what it was. Her face went white when she saw the Nazi insignia. Aunt Lucy did not speak or read German so did not know what it said; however, she read the clue and carefully replaced the paper back where she had found it and went down stairs to find Uncle Josh.

What do you make of the clue?
Do you think the children should perhaps involve an adult now that it appears to be getting rather serious?
Do you have someone you confide in? It may not be a person; it may be a special keepsake like Ella has in Horace.
Have you ever said you were doing something but in fact have been doing something entirely different?

Chapter 19

After crossing several more roads and passing the very impressive Government House, the children reached a large church on the top of the hill, which they knew must be St Saviour's. They entered the grounds through the large lych-gate and walked up the narrow pathway to the church passing gravestones and large tombs en route. They looked very old and you could barely see the writing etched into most of them.

The crenelated tower rose up before them and a large clock face with roman numerals dominated the front wall of the tower. The building was made of large blocks of stone and had beautiful arched windows of stained glass on either side of the vestibule, which was in front of the tower.

Ella was the first to notice the gargoyles on the top of the tower but only on three corners, one having been broken off over time.

The gravestones lay all around the churchyard as far as the eye could see.

"So where do we start?" said Marcus looking around rather bewildered.

"I suggest we split up," said James. "That gives us a better chance of covering a large area, as we don't have much time."

"Right, good idea," said Marcus. "I Googled Lillie Langtry's grave and it showed a picture of a bust as the top of the headstone."

"A bust!" exclaimed Ella shocked.

"A bust is a statue of a person but only the head and shoulders," said James.

"Oh," said Ella, feeling a bit embarrassed.

"It is supposedly a bust of her, Lillie herself and it is in white marble, so it should not be that difficult to spot," added Marcus.

"Okay, let's get going," said James. "I'll take the right side, Marcus, you and Ella take the left-hand side as it is a larger space."

Splitting up, they started their search for Lillie's resting place. Ella walked along the pathway turning right and Marcus continued straight crossing over a pathway onto another. There were graves and tombs either side. Some of them very old indeed, as you could no longer read the inscriptions on them as the weather had worn them away. The churchyard was very well kept as the grass that grew between each gravestone was neatly clipped and the graves themselves were obviously attended to. There was the odd bunch of flowers placed here and there, but for the most part, there was just the main tombstones sticking out or flat marble slabs to indicate the grave below.

Ella stopped to read the ones she could and noticed that they dated back to the 19th century; some just had a name and the dates that the person had lived or died, others named several people who must also be buried in the same grave. Short verses or prayers were scribed on various headstones, which were quite sad to read. Ella had never been into a cemetery before and found it all quite fascinating.

She continued on the pathway and then abruptly stopped, there on the tombstone on her right was a magpie, its black eyes watching her, it hopped down onto the grave where two other magpies joined it. Ella's heart was thumping. She watched cautiously as the birds seemed to be waiting for something. They hopped and fluttered around then in a flash they rose into the air and flew further down the path where they appeared to settle on another grave. Ella followed swiftly; sure enough, they had landed on a large tomb. Before she knew it, three more magpies joined the group and they all fluttered and squawked.

"Six," Ella said to herself. "Six for gold." *They know where the treasure is,* she thought to herself.

Ella so wanted the boys to be there, as she felt a bit nervous, she looked around her and then she saw it. There was a grave with a head on a stone plinth. She hurried across to it and standing in front, she noticed there was another headstone behind. This was it, Lillie Langtry's grave the name was clearly etched on the headstone. As soon as she had reached it, the magpies rose into the air and flew away over the cemetery.

Ella quickly darted back up the pathway and seeing James in the distance waved her arms vigorously, not wanting to shout as this was a cemetery after all. It seemed like ages but eventually James noticed her and came hurrying over.

"I have found it, it's down this way," she said breathlessly, pointing in the direction she had come.

James told her to stay where she was while he fetched Marcus.

When the boys came back, they all went to view Lillie's grave. Someone had laid a bunch of beautiful pink lilies on the grave; they looked very fresh and must have been put there that morning.

"Well done, Ella," said Marcus.

"It actually wasn't me that found it," said Ella. "I had help from a group of magpies."

The boys looked at her incredulously.

"What?" said James in disbelief.

Marcus was very quiet; he knew that someone was helping them and he knew exactly whom it was.

Ella explained, "There were six of them, as the rhyme goes it is six for gold."

As if on cue the magpies reappeared, they swooped down over the children and landed on the pathway. They hopped and fluttered only this time Ella counted eight.

"Eight, what's that for," said Marcus.

Ella couldn't think, she quickly recited the rhyme to herself and then blurted out, "It's for a wish."

"Well, we wish to find the soldiers grave in the clue," said Marcus.

As soon as Marcus had spoken, two magpies hopped onto Lillie Langtry's grave. They eyed the children with their black beady eyes then flew over the hedge that lay behind the grave and swooped down onto a grave behind.

"Two for joy," said Ella. "I think you will find that the grave we want is on the other side of the hedge."

The children could not go through the hedge so they raced back down the pathway to where they could walk through to the other side. They then went to see where the magpies were. Sure enough, they had settled on a grave and were pecking at the grass. There was no headstone just a stone frame around the grave. On the left side of this stone frame was a name etched in black, James read it out. **Siegfried Carl Hans Albert Theobald Zimmerman.**

"Crikey," said Marcus, "that's a mouthful."

"Isn't that a German name," said Ella. "I think we may have found our soldier."

On the right-hand side of the frame was his date of birth 1894 and the year in which he had died 1945.

"It doesn't say anything about him being a soldier," said James.

"Wait a minute," said Marcus. "Look at this." The children bent down to see where Marcus was pointing. The bottom left hand edge, just under the name, the words **SS Oberfuhrer Schweiger** had been carefully chiselled into the stonework. The lettering was no bigger than a centimetre and was partially hidden by the grass.

"I do think we have our soldier and I think the treasure is in the grave," said Marcus.

"We need to think about all this very carefully, but now we must get back to the cinema before it is discovered that we didn't see any film," said James, looking at his watch.

James took a few photos of the grave with his mobile. As the children made their way out of the churchyard, a parliament of magpies rose into the air squawking and chirping as they headed to the nearby trees.

The walk back to St Helier was much quicker as it was downhill all the way. James happened to mention how odd it was that the magpies had been there. Ella was convinced that they had helped them. James thought this was a ridiculous notion. Marcus was very quiet. He wondered whether this was the right time to tell James and Ella about the Faerie Queen. So, he relayed how he had obtained the last clue and how the Queen had seemed to evaporate before his very eyes. He also told them that she wanted payment in kind and that they had to do something to preserve nature on the island. When he had finished James said, "You've got to be kidding me, faeries what are you going to tell me next, Marcus?"

Ella was quite indignant. "Well, James, I believe Marcus," she said. "I know that Maud believes in faerie folk too. They are not the cute little things that flit about flowers. They are a type of spirit that protects nature and yes, they can change their form and can help us humans and they can also harm us. The old man and woman we saw are faeries and were there to help us, as did the magpies."

"I am sorry," said James. "I just find it all so surreal."

"There is no need to tell anyone else about all this," said Marcus. "What we have to worry about now is how we get the treasure and I am convinced that there is treasure here on the island and it is in that grave."

James agreed their priority was to get the treasure. They walked on in silence everyone wondering what they should do next. They managed to reach the cinema in plenty of time and waited patiently for Uncle Josh. When he arrived, he explained that he would take them all to Spud End as Marcus and James were being picked up from there.

On the way back, Uncle Josh was unusually quiet and did not ask anything about the film, which the children found surprising.

As they drew up outside the house, James noticed his mum's blue mini in the driveway and Marcus saw his dad's black VW golf there too. They thought this was a bit odd because normally one parent would have taken both the boys as they lived close to each other.

This unfortunately was not the only surprise that awaited them as seated in the lounge were both Marcus's and James's parents. Aunt Lucy gave them all some lemonade and then Alison asked how the film was. James hastily said it was great and Marcus added he had been scared stiff at one point when the T Rex was on the loose.

"That is surprising," said Alison calmly as the cinema was closed this afternoon due to a technical fault.

The children froze. Ella wanted the ground to swallow her up and could feel her cheeks getting redder.

"Now," said Tom, "please can you tell us what is going on. You are all up to something and we need to know the full story."

Ella decided as she was the one that had really started it all she should be the one to explain.

Ella began by telling them how they had found a clue at the tower, which led them to Gorey castle. From there how they had found another clue which took them to Devil's Hole. She did not mention the black dog or the old couple and certainly not how Marcus had obtained the clue at Devil's Hole. She felt there were some things adults would just never understand. She did mention how Maud had been really helpful, as she knew more about the island than anyone else they knew. Today they had gone in search of Lillie Langtry's tomb trying to follow the last clue.

The adults listened in silence then Aunt Lucy admitted that she had found the clue in Horace's jacket and was seriously worried as she saw the Nazi insignia which had also been on the pouch that Ella had left on the bed. She was responsible for calling everyone together.

Uncle Josh, who had been deep in thought, suddenly, said he had heard that there was treasure on the island. He was of the understanding that when the Germans occupied the Channel Islands during the Second World War, they brought precious items, paintings and jewellery that sort of things from Europe and stashed it here on Jersey. Tom also agreed with Josh saying he too had heard similar stories.

Penny, Marcus's mum, was annoyed with the children and told them how irresponsible they had been. She for one was worried, as anything could have happened to them. On the other hand, she had to admit she was very proud of the fact that they had worked together and managed to solve these clues.

"Right," said Tom. "What do we do next? Well, I think we need to sit together and work out the best way forward as you have come so far with this. Of course, you understand this could all be a hoax and come to nothing?" he said.

Aunt Lucy asked Alison and Penny if they would help her to rustle up something for supper. They agreed and disappeared into the kitchen. Greg, Tom and Josh sat with the children as they wanted to know more about what the children had discovered that afternoon on their illicit trip to St Saviour's.

Have you ever been caught out doing something you thought nobody else knew you were doing?
Have you ever visited a graveyard or cemetery and looked at the different gravestones and tombs?
Do you think that perhaps this is now the right time to get parents involved in the search for the treasure?

Chapter 20

Later that evening, they all sat around the large farmhouse kitchen table tucking into a feast that the mums and Aunt Lucy had put together. A large hock of cooked smoked ham, boiled eggs, a pasta salad, a green salad, sliced beetroot in vinegar, coleslaw and lots of crusty bread and creamy butter and of course a large bowl of small, warm, home grown new potatoes.

The conversation naturally centred on the treasure and Greg and Tom were very interested in seeing Maud to find out what she knew about the war days. They also told the children that as Tom was on holiday, he would take the children tomorrow down to the library and research the archives to see what they could tell them about the German occupation. They would also have to speak to the rector of St Saviour's church and see what he knew about this grave, which by all accounts had the body of Siegfried Carl Hans Albert Theobald Zimmerman in.

Aunt Lucy was just about to serve some apple pie and ice cream for dessert when Jenny and Art arrived. They had actually not come to eat but seeing as everyone was there, they decided to stay. They had Bailey with them who was just beside himself with so many people to lick and jump on.

Art and Jenny were found chairs and managed to squeeze themselves around the table and were filled in as to what was going on. Jenny was quite shocked to hear the children had taken themselves off to St Saviour's cemetery by themselves. She told them she would have taken them if they had only asked. Art, on the other hand, was fascinated with the idea of treasure here on Jersey, he had never heard of anything like that. Greg picked up the clue in German and nonchalantly said they needed to get that translated.

"Oh! I speak German," said Jenny.

Everyone looked at her in amazement.

"My father worked for I.C.I and we as a family were sent to live in Germany for three years and I went to a German school."

"Can you translate this," said Greg handing Jenny the clue.

"Let's see," she said. Peering at the paper, she started, "...Zimmermann is dead...The rest of us have to leave the island tomorrow. The treasure is well hidden...Only four of us now know the...Now what is 'standort'?" she asked herself biting her lower lip as she thought.

"Ah! Yes, it's location. Only four of us now know the...location...We will come back and...*zu bekommen, zu bekommen*...what is that now...erm, er...get it...ah! Now I know it...find a way to get it. Helmut Schatz."

"Excellent," said Tom. That is really helpful. This chap Helmut Schatz must have written this clue before he left the island.

"Well, that's the funny thing," said Jenny. "The name Helmut Schatz, it can't be his real name, you see...*schatz* in German means treasure."

They all stared at her open mouthed.

"Are you sure about that," said Uncle Josh.

"Absolutely," she said.

"Ah! so then," said James excitedly, "Siegfried Carl Hans Albert Theobald Zimmerman is not a real person either, look," he pointed out, "the first letter of each name, it spells out *schatz*."

"I told you," said Marcus, "the treasure is in that grave."

"Well spotted," said Uncle Josh in amazement.

"So, it is the other name we must focus on," said Greg. "This SS Oberfuhrer Schweiger, he must have been some sort of commander in the German forces."

"He was SS," explained Tom. "Not a nice bunch at all, he would have been responsible for keeping order on the island."

"You mean a policeman?" said Ella.

"Not really," said Tom.

Aunt Lucy butted in to say would anyone like any more to eat as she was about to clear away.

"I think it's time to leave all this until tomorrow," said Greg. Everyone was a bit tired especially after such a plentiful supper.

Tom agreed he would help the children in the morning, as he was the only dad that was on holiday and therefore had the time.

"Let me have a good think about all this." he said, "and let's see what tomorrow brings."

Can you speak another language?

Would you have told the adults about the faeries or the disappearing people?

What sort of treasure do you think may be in the grave?

Chapter 21

Ella lay in bed that night tingling with excitement. She wasn't the least bit sleepy. So much was going on in her head. An awful thought crossed her mind too that she had less than ten days to go as her stay on Jersey was coming to an end. Aunt Lucy had decided to travel back to England with her so she could see her father and her sister, Ella's mum.

It seemed to Ella that they were very close to finding the treasure. She hated to think that if they did find it, she would miss out on all excitement.

When she got up the next morning, Aunt Lucy told her Tom had called and that he was going to collect her around ten and with the boys, they were going to see the rector of St Saviour's church. Ella wolfed down a piece of toast and a boiled egg and got herself ready to go. It seemed like hours but was all of thirty minutes that she waited before Tom drew up outside in his black VW Golf.

On the way to St Saviour's church, Tom told the children that he had called the rector and asked if they could come and view a grave in the cemetery. He had not said why. The rector was pleased to show them around and agreed to meet them. The drive to the church seemed to take forever but on arrival, the Very Reverend Michael Hambly was there to meet them. He was a very jolly man, rather tubby with rosy cheeks and a welcoming smile on his face. He was dressed in his cassock, and his white wispy hair blew uncontrollably in the breeze.

He introduced himself to them all and told the children to call him Michael. He then ushered them into the church where they sat down on a pew.

"Now," he said, "what can I do to help you?"

Tom told him they were interested in a particular grave. He also went on to explain why they were interested. The Very Reverend Michael was amazed to hear their tale, but he told them that every grave in the churchyard was numbered and the contents of each one recorded so he was able to check for them. He asked them to come with him into the vestry.

Michael produced a large map of the cemetery with all the graves marked and numbered.

"Firstly, you need to show me which one it is," he told them as he lay the large map down on a wooden table.

The children poured over the map trying to get their bearings.

"It's this one," said James eventually pointing to a grave on the map. "I'm pretty sure."

"Let's take a look," said Michael as he put on his spectacles. "That is near to Lillie Langtry's grave," he said as he pointed out her grave too.

"Yes, yes," said Marcus excitedly. "That's it."

"Right, now I just need to take the number and I will tell you who lies in it."

He meticulously wrote down the information on a piece of paper and then went over to his laptop, which was lying on top of a large wooden cupboard.

The children waited anxiously; Marcus convinced that the treasure was in the grave.

"Now that is odd," said Michael after a few minutes. "That plot according to the records was taken in March 1945 by SS Oberfuhrer Schweiger."

"That is the name on the grave," said Marcus.

"But that can't be so," replied Michael. "You see the German military were all buried in a German War Cemetery at St Brelade. None were permitted in this graveyard."

"I told you," said Marcus, "the treasure is in that grave."

"Let's not run before we can walk," said his father. "We need to make sure that we have all the facts before we start making any statements about treasure."

"To be perfectly honest," said the Very Reverend Michael looking at the children, "the grave is very small, you won't get a lot of treasure in there. If you were thinking of a hiding place for treasure, I suppose it is a good one but for a very small hoard."

He went on to tell the children that he had heard many stories about the treasure and was of the belief that if there was any, it was a vast amount. These would have been paintings and valuable objects taken from museums and art galleries in Europe.

The children hadn't quite imagined what this treasure could be and suddenly listening to Michael, they realised maybe it was a large amount and could well be hidden somewhere else.

Michael saw the disappointment on their faces and hastily said, "Leave it with me for a few days and I will make some further inquiries about this grave and get back to you."

Tom thanked Michael for all his help and told the children they would head to the Library next and see what the archive section had to reveal. They needed to find out who this Oberfuhrer Schweiger really was and if he had existed at all.

"How about we stop off at McDonald's?" said Tom. "Or is no one hungry?"

The children didn't say no to that and as they were seated with their cokes and Big Macs and fries, they started to feel a bit more positive.

"Look at it this way," said James, "the grave is dodgy, as Michael doesn't seem to think that a German soldier should be in it, so something isn't right."

"Yes," agreed Marcus, "and Oberfuhrer Schweiger must have died just as the Germans were leaving as liberation day is 9th May. That is if he was a real person."

"There are a lot of unanswered questions," said Tom. "We need to get all the facts before we make any rash statements."

Ella sat quietly munching her fries, she reckoned that they wouldn't have been helped this far if there wasn't something at the end of it. She was convinced there was treasure and that the grave was a key to getting it.

Have you ever been convinced of something and then found out that you were wrong?

How would you feel if you were Ella?

What do you think would be part of this treasure?

Chapter 22

On entering the library, they made their way to the archive department, which was up three flights of stairs. When they arrived, they found a very young receptionist sitting at a desk. Tom politely told her that they were making inquiries about the German officers that were in charge of the island in 1945 before liberation day.

The young girl eyed them up and down and then said rather tersely, "Why do you want to know that?"

Tom smiled and calmly told her that the children were doing a project on the liberation of the Channel Islands.

"Well, the person you want to speak to is Mr Gobrey, he knows all about those sort of things," she answered. "I'll see if he is available." She then disappeared through a doorway.

Within minutes, Mr Gobrey appeared, he was a middle aged, thin, wiry looking man with dark slicked back hair. His nose and chin were quite pointed and Ella thought he looked like a human version of a goblin from Harry Potter's Gringott's Bank. He was however, charming and when Tom told him what they wanted, he was delighted to help. He appeared very knowledgeable about the liberation of the islands and informed the children and Tom that a man called Graf von Schmettow was the military commander in chief of the troops on the Channel Islands until February 1945 when Vice Admiral Hüffmeier then took command.

Tom asked him about SS Oberfuhrer Schweiger. Mr Gobrey had not heard of him but mentioned there were several SS men that came and went during the occupation. He explained that the title Uberfuhrer meant senior leader and had the ranking of a colonel. He would have been someone of importance and being in the SS meant he was involved with intelligence, policing and security. They represented the Nazi party. He made a note of the name and said he would investigate for them. He then took the children downstairs to the history section of the library and showed them some very interesting books about the occupation of the Channel Islands between 1940 and 1945 by the German Forces.

Later in the car, on their way back to Spud End, Marcus mentioned how helpful Mr Gobrey had been showing them all these books about the war and how it had affected the islanders. Some of the books were quite detailed with old photographs. James remembered seeing a photograph in one book of a German Officer talking to a British policeman how strange it seemed that both the uniforms were pictured together. After all, they were enemies. They realised how difficult life must have been for the islanders having German soldiers everywhere. Ella too had been fascinated and wondered how her uncle's family had managed with their farm through it all.

As Tom dropped Ella off, he told them all that now they just had to be patient and play the waiting game. He assured them that it wouldn't be long before they got some answers; in the meantime, they were just to wait and not attempt to get more clues or do things by themselves. They all agreed.

The waiting for the children seemed to take ages, but less than four days later, the Very Reverend Michael Hambly called Tom. He did indeed have some good news, which Tom was pleased to relay to the children, Greg and Josh. Michael explained that he had informed the authorities of the grave and that it held a German soldier by all accounts. They had insisted that the body, if it was a German soldier, had to be removed and sent back to the deceased person's homeland, which naturally was Germany. He was arranging with the Environmental Health Officer for Jersey to get a special license so that the coffin could be exhumed. The forensic scientists could then identify the remains and return them to the next of kin in Germany. Of course, this was not something that could be done easily as there was a lot of paper work involved, but he promised to let Tom know when the coffin would be exhumed.

This delighted the children especially Marcus who was still convinced that there was treasure in the grave.

Jenny had arranged for the children, Tom and Greg to see Maud. Jenny had told her a bit about the children finding clues to the treasure and she was very eager to speak to them. It was late one Wednesday afternoon that they all went round for tea. This time Greg had a splendid Victoria Sandwich cake, which had been baked that morning filled with homemade strawberry jam and rich Jersey cream. He had heard the story of how Maud had been at school with his grandfather and was delighted to meet her. She was her normal perky self, her cold completely gone even so Jenny made her sit and entertain her guests while she made the tea and served the cake.

As Jenny disappeared into the kitchen, Greg asked Maud if she remembered anything about the war. Maud explained she was a young girl in her early teens when the Germans took over the island. She explained it was difficult, as they had all felt sorry for the young soldiers who had to patrol the island and were away from their own families. The islanders would often speak in 'Jerriais', which is a form of French and only understood by the islanders.

She also told them a story about one dark night when a soldier asked the way to the boat yard. One of the islanders told him to just walk straight and then turn right when he saw a cement boulder and to keep going and he would find his way. Of course, there were no lights. The poor soldier kept walking and walking and eventually he walked right off the pier into the cold water below. He was fine after the ordeal just very shocked and of course very wet. The islanders just revelled in it thinking it was a huge joke.

Greg asked her if she knew who the commander was. Maud had a story to tell about him too. She said she remembered one day when she had been out shopping with her mum, not that there was a lot to buy as food was scarce, but her young sister was with her. They were walking down to the harbour where there was a wet fish shop as her mum was hoping to get some shellfish to make into a broth. Her sister was carrying her soft teddy and was swinging it around when it fell into the gutter. Just at that moment, a large German staff car drew up alongside and almost drove over the bear that was lying in the road. Her sister screamed and started to cry. The driver got out of the car and opened the passenger door to let out a man in a uniform. They were petrified, as he looked so stern and important. He bent down and picked the teddy bear up and dusted it off then turning to her sister, he kindly gave it to her with a smile. Her sister was so happy to get her teddy back she said nothing but Maud thanked the man who smiled and nodded at her. Maud later found out this was the commandant. Maud added that he had a reputation of being very strict, but he was also very fair, kind and thoughtful to all the islanders. Greg told her this must have been Graf von Schmettow.

Jenny had been busy bringing in the tea and cake whilst Maud told her story. They sat enjoying the soft spongy cake with the sweet jam and delicious cream whilst Maud talked about the hospital that the Germans built on the island for the wounded soldiers. Her father had been a doctor and was told by the Germans to work there. She said he never talked about it although she knew that boats would come in and the injured men would be taken to the hospital. Jenny told her it was now a tourist attraction and was very popular as it was very well preserved looking as it had done in the war years. Maud tut-tutted and shook her head; she certainly didn't approve of visiting that place.

Suddenly, Tom's mobile rang making them all jump. He also was quite surprised and quickly located it in his jacket pocket.

"Hello," he said. "Yes, speaking. Oh! Hello, how good of you to get back to me so quickly." He then paused and listened.

"I see," he went on. "Oh! Really, that is interesting, yes thank you very much, Mr Gobrey, you have been very thorough and I am very grateful. I will certainly get back to you and thank you once again."

"Well, well, well," said Tom as he slipped his mobile back into his jacket pocket.

Everyone looked at Tom and Ella held her breath, as she just knew something important was coming.

"So, what did Mr Gobrey have to say, Dad," asked Marcus excitedly.

Tom smiled and told them all that Mr Gobrey had been making inquiries about Oberfuhrer Schweiger. It appears he was on Jersey for a time but fled before the island was liberated. He went to France where he was caught by the allies and tried for war crimes. He died in Germany in 1982.

"So," said Ella in a soft voice, "whose body is in the grave in St Saviour's churchyard?"

"That," said Tom, "is what we are about to find out when the coffin is exhumed tomorrow."

Do you think it was kind to play tricks on people even if they are the enemy and occupying your land?
Why do you think the German Army had a military hospital on the island of Jersey?
What do you think they will find in the coffin when they exhume it?

Chapter 23

"The process for exhuming a body is a very difficult and complicated matter," explained Greg who had been making inquiries with the Very Reverend Michael Hambly. "Firstly, you have to have a very special casket made to put the original coffin in."

"In what way special?" asked James.

"Well, it has to be lead lined for a start and there are a lot of other restrictions on what has to be done. The Environmental Health Officer is involved in making sure everything is done correctly," answered Greg. "The whole procedure takes time as you have to obtain a license from The Ministry of Justice and that normally costs a lot of money. You also have to seek permission from the bishop if it is to be undertaken in a churchyard."

"Where do they take the body," asked Marcus.

"In this case, it will go to the police forensic department as they have to find out just whose body it is."

The children listened intently.

Greg went on to say finally the Very Reverend Michael Hambly had got all the necessary papers and approvals together. He had been intrigued by the fact that a German soldier had ended up in St Saviour's cemetery and he was eager to solve the mystery. Greg had been helping him and they had gone through all the church archives but could find nothing that had given permission for the coffin to be buried in that plot.

"I suppose," said Greg with a sigh, "as it was war time, a lot of things went by the by and regular rules were broken."

The next day, Thursday, was very wet and windy, not a typical August day at all. The Environmental Health Officer, the Cemetery's Officer, the Very Reverend Michael Hambly, two policemen and two gravediggers all assembled at 9.30 a.m. sharp around the graveside of this unknown person in St Saviour's churchyard. Michael said a quick prayer before the gravediggers commenced their work and of course affirmed to the Environmental Health Officer that this indeed was the plot that needed investigating.

Once the outer stone frame had been removed, the gravediggers dug down till their shovels hit something firm. They cleared the soil away and then prepared the new casket that was large enough to take the one in the grave. They carefully managed to raise up the coffin and with guidance from the Cemetery's Officer and careful precision, they placed it in the big open casket.

The Environmental Officer watched everything closely making sure the new casket was sealed and a plaque was placed on the top with an identification number clearly written on it. It was his job to make sure everything was carried out hygienically. He also oversaw that there was nothing else in the grave and that everywhere sanitised. All this was undertaken in a dignified and respectful manner. The Very Reverend Michael Hambly watched the entire event in silence, his mind intently on the poor soul of the departed man in the coffin.

The sealed casket was taken away by a police van to the forensic lab, as it was there it would be reopened and the forensic scientist would hopefully be able to identify the remains.

The whole event took just over an hour and was decidedly miserable as the drizzling rain persisted and the wind blew relentlessly making everyone feel cold and very uncomfortable. The Very Reverend Michael Hambly happened to look up for a split second during the proceedings as they were digging the earth away. He saw two people sheltering under the tree at the side of the cemetery about two hundred yards away, it was an old man with a white beard and spectacles who was wearing a grey plastic mac and was holding an umbrella. Standing with him was an old woman with a funny cloche hat; she also was wearing a plastic mac. They seemed to be staring over at him. Michael glanced down to watch as the gravediggers found the coffin and started to dig around it. When he looked up again, the odd couple had gone. Looking around, he could see no sign of them. *How very odd,* he thought. They just seemed to disappear and then he turned his attentions once again onto the grim exercise he was witnessing.

When the unattractive job was completed, they all went back to Michael's house just across from the churchyard where his wife supplied very welcoming mugs of steaming tea and some shortbread biscuits. It wasn't long before they were all feeling a good deal better.

Michael called Greg to let him know that everything had gone well and that the forensic report would probably be available the following week.

Ella was hoping the following week would not come as it was her last week with her Aunt and Uncle, as much as she loved her parents, she desperately wanted to know what the forensic scientists would find out. She also knew that she would miss Spud End and of course the boys and Jenny.

During her last week, everyone was so kind. Penny, Marcus's mum, arranged to take her and the boys to Corbiere lighthouse, which was built on a headland out in the sea. It was quite an amazing feature standing on a rugged strip of rock watching over the ragged coastline as the waves came crashing in sending an ever-ending stream of spray onto the surrounding shore line. Ella thought it was magnificent standing majestically looking out over the rough waves.

Another day, Alison, James's mum, took her and the boys out to lunch at the crab shack again and then they went to see the sandcastle man who created the most amazing sand castles and palaces. Ella had never seen anything like it. There was a fabulous fairy tale castle with turrets and towers with a winding road to its entrance, a fierce dragon draped around a brick wall and even a handsome prince not to mention a splendid eagle. It was just brilliant. She could not believe it was all made entirely out of sand. The man who built it was known on the island as the sand wizard and Ella believed he must be to work such magic with just sand.

Jenny also had a surprise for her on Friday, with Art and Maud in her wheelchair; they went to see the Battle of Flowers. They watched the parade as it made its way along Victoria Avenue. Ella did not think she had ever seen so many vibrant colours together; the flowers were just amazing. The islanders had been very creative, there was a float with Captain Hook on and another with a giant clown fish, there was even a Viking boat. All the floats were covered in beautiful coloured flowers. Lots of young girls dressed in exotic costumes walked with the parade. It was a truly spectacular sight.

Ella also found time in the last week to help Aunt Lucy and Uncle Josh on the farm potato picking, which she loved even though it was hard work. The best bit was it worked up an appetite and Ella couldn't wait to get back to the farm to see what delights Aunt Lucy had prepared for the hungry work force.

It had been a very special and eventful last week of her stay and the only disappointment for Ella was that she was not able to find the treasure, which she had dreamt of doing. It was while she was packing her case ready to leave that her Aunt called her to come downstairs quickly. Uncle Josh was on the phone to Tom. When he finished, he asked Ella to sit down at the kitchen table and with Aunt Lucy and a glass of homemade lemonade; he explained what had happened.

The forensic scientist had managed to identify the corpse in the coffin. It was not Oberfuhrer Schweiger, which they already knew. It was a German man called Hermann Lechner.

"How on earth did they find that out," said Ella.

"Well," said Uncle Josh, "from his skull they were able to build his face so they then knew what he looked like. From that, they started investigating old military documents and before long discovered who he was. They knew he had been on Jersey, his uniform and military records showed he was an Unteroffizier, which in our army is a sergeant. His skeletal remains showed signs that he had been badly wounded. They think he was a patient in the German hospital who had been brought from France to be treated."

"So, what was he doing in the grave?" questioned Ella.

"Well, that is the interesting part," said Uncle Josh. "They think that he may have died in the hospital and his body was used to hide something. That is how he got to be buried in St Saviour's churchyard."

"What could he possibly hide if he was dead," said Ella perplexed.

"There was something else they found too. It was a black notebook in the left breast pocket of his uniform. When the forensic scientist read it, he couldn't believe his eyes. It was a list of artefacts that are virtually priceless and where they could be found."

Ella looked at her Aunt and Uncle.

"Are you saying it was the treasure," she said excitedly.

"It certainly seems like it," said Uncle Josh smiling, and you and the boys take all the credit for finding it.

"Well, they have to see if it is where it says it is," added her Aunt, "but it does all look very positive, we will know for sure next week as they are going to see if they can retrieve it all."

"But I will be gone by then," sighed Ella.

"Don't worry about that," said Uncle Josh giving her a hug. "You can always come back and stay here, but I think now your mum and dad would like to see you."

"Where is it," stammered Ella.

"They would not say, but be sure they will let us know as soon as they find anything."

"So, what will happen now to the corpse?" asked Ella.

"Well, now they know who he is they will make sure he is returned to his relatives in Germany, they should have no problem tracing the next of kin and he will have a resting place back in his homeland," said Aunt Lucy.

Ella was disappointed she would not be there when they found the treasure but on the other hand knew that she needed to get back to her parents. After all, it was less than an hour away by plane. She also reckoned Marcus would be pleased as he said the treasure was in the grave and indirectly it was.

The next day, Saturday, Aunt Lucy and Ella arrived at Jersey airport for their flight to Cardiff. Uncle Josh took them in the battered old Range Rover. As they approached departures, there was Marcus with his parents Penny and Tom and James with his parents Alison and Greg. They had all come to wish them a good flight.

Ella thanked them all for a wonderful time and promised to come back soon. James and Marcus said they would stay in touch with her and let her know what was happening. As they were about to go through, there was a shout and Jenny came running over with Bailey in tow. Breathlessly, she handed Ella a little gift.

"Something to remind you of Jersey," she said, "but I have no doubt I will see you very soon." After more hugs and kisses, they went through to the gate and soon after boarded the aircraft.

After an uneventful flight, they landed bang on time in Cardiff and there was her mum to meet her. She was naturally delighted to see Ella and her sister Lucy and threw her arms around Ella first and then hugged Aunt Lucy. On the way back home in the car, her mum talked about how well her grandfather was doing with his new hip and how he was really getting about now a lot better than before. Ella's mind was still in Jersey recalling all the wonderful things she had done in the four weeks of her stay. Sometime she would tell her mother about it, but for now, she needed to settle back into life in her own home.

How would you feel after coming back from a wonderful holiday?
Where do you think the treasure is hidden?
What sort of artefacts do you think might be included in the treasure?

Chapter 24

Ella's grandfather had made a remarkable recovery and was managing splendidly with his new hip. He was very interested in hearing all about Ella's trip to Spud End and Ella was happy to explain to him all about her hunt for treasure with the boys. She told him all about Maud and how she had helped them as she knew all about the island. She explained how they worked out the clues and the trail they followed to eventually get to the graveyard. Grandpa knew all about Lillie Langtry and said if he ever got to Jersey again, he would certainly like to see her grave. Ella refrained from mentioning the old couple or the faeries as she felt he would perhaps not have taken her seriously.

Ella's brother Tom was his usual self although thankfully he was hardly there. His little holiday job kept him very busy. He disappeared off to work before Ella came down for breakfast each morning so it was only in the evening, she saw him. He was full of himself and with the fact that he had earned some money. He bored everyone senseless talking about the technical things he planned to buy with it. Ella thought anyone would think he was a millionaire the way he carried on.

With only another week to go before Ella had to return to school, she decided that she needed to get herself organised. She got up early on the Monday morning and went down to breakfast with every intention of coming back upstairs to sort out her books and papers ready for school.

She sat down at the table for breakfast opposite Aunt Lucy. Her father was as usual hidden behind his paper engrossed in the finance pages. Ella gratefully took a slice of toast from her mother and was just reaching for the butter, when her eyes fell on the front page of her father's newspaper. It read 'Amazing Find on Jersey', Ella's heart nearly missed a beat.

"Aunt Lucy, look," she gasped.

The paper came down with a crackle.

"What in heaven's name is going on?" said her father.

Aunt Lucy grabbed the paper out of his hands and turning to the front page started reading the text out load.

"Treasure has been found at a tourist attraction used by the German military during the war. Acting on information received the Lieutenant Governor of Jersey informed reporters that this was indeed an exceptional find. He said it is an amazing hoard, which at the moment appeared to be worth at a rough estimate more than two million pounds."

At this point, Aunt Lucy had to stop and take a deep breath.

"The treasure had been hidden away behind a false wall in the old military hospital. The Lieutenant Governor explained the items all had to be sorted and catalogued, and that some of them returned to where they originally came from. When asked by reporters how they came to know of the treasure, the lieutenant governor announced it had been the work of three children."

It then listed some of the things they had found. Ella's dad read it out, "There were paintings by the impressionists Degas, Monet and Renoir. A canvas of Klimt's work perfectly preserved, of a village by the sea. There were a couple of statues of Gods or athletes these were thought to be from Ancient Greece or Rome. There was one unique statue sculpted by James Pradier. They found a collection of Faberge decorated eggs, wonderful art deco porcelain vases hand painted by Goldscheider, glassware by Lalique, exquisite jewellery by Cartier and Boucheron as well as pearls, necklaces and bracelets by Wartski. There was even a wooden case of first edition leather bound books. The main find were two paintings by Arnold Bocklin, said to be Hitler's favourite artist, which were neatly stacked and well preserved."

When Ella's father had finished, there was stunned silence.

Aunt Lucy sat down. "I can't believe it," she said. "Ella, this is all down to you, James and Marcus. I have to ring Josh and find out what has been happening." She got up and went to call on her mobile.

Ella was stunned and inside her tummy, she felt it was just full of butterflies; she was so excited, she really didn't know what to say. Her father and mother who knew something about her treasure hunting but didn't take it seriously were full of admiration.

"Oh, Ella," said her mother, "this is truly wonderful, I can't believe you were responsible for finding something so amazing."

"You know, Ella," said her father, "to find these wonderful works of art that have been hidden away for so many years will bring a lot of happiness to a number of people. They will now be able to view these treasures and see these fantastic works. I am really very proud of you."

Aunt Lucy came back to say that the treasure was only found late yesterday afternoon. Someone had leaked it to the press, which is why it had hit the headlines. Uncle Josh had said the whole island is in uproar and swarming with press and television people.

Grandpa suddenly noticed a small group of people outside the front door. Within minutes, the doorbell rang. Ella's father went to see who it was.

They could hear him saying yes, an Ella Johnson does live here but it was not convenient to speak with her at the moment. Yes, he added, she was one of the children that had helped to find the treasure.

"I think," said Grandpa, "you have suddenly become very famous."

Ella blushed; she was not so sure she liked that.

"How on earth did they know where she lived?" said Ella's mum.

"In the world we live in today it's not difficult to find anyone if you really want to," said Ella's dad as he came back to finish his breakfast. "I think I will have another cup of tea," he said offering his mug to Ella's mum and promptly picking up his newspaper, he shook it to try and get the creases out and sat down to read where he left off.

That morning, the phone did not stop ringing and Ella was told it was best if she didn't venture out as there were several photographers waiting at the front gate for a snap shot of her.

Ella carried on doing what she had set out to do that day but managed to have a SKYPE call with James and Marcus and their parents with Aunt Lucy and her mum. They explained all that had happened.

Two days later, Ella received an invitation from the Lieutenant Governor to visit Jersey as they wished to thank her along with her friends in a public ceremony.

This sent her mother into a panic as she said she would have to get her something nice to wear. Aunt Lucy said they could all stay at Spud End and so arrangements were made. Ella was just delighted to be going back to Jersey so soon. She wasn't sure what she was going to be doing, but it would be good to see everyone again and to go this time with her mum and dad.

How would you feel suddenly becoming famous and in the public eye?
Where do you think all these art treasures have come from?
Do you think Ella and the boys will get a reward?

Chapter 25

The following Friday, Ella and her family were at Spud End in Jersey, even her brother had agreed to come. He admired the potato farm and Uncle Josh said next year he could come and work there and have a holiday at the same time. Tom was really chuffed as Uncle Josh let him drive the potato picker only in the fields of course, but Tom thought this was great.

On the Saturday, there was a lunch at Government House to meet the Lieutenant Governor and his wife plus his staff. He wanted to hear all about how they had found the treasure. Not only were the children invited but their families and friends too. Aunt Lucy and Uncle Josh plus Jenny, Art and of course Maud who had played a major role in helping them. The Very Reverend Michael Hambly and his wife Vivian also joined them delighted to be part of this auspicious occasion.

The children had agreed on a story, as they did not want to mention the faeries and their involvement. James in particular was very sceptical of the whole thing. They explained how they had found the clues and how they had needed help to interpret them.

Before lunch, a video of how they broke a wall down at the old German hospital was shown. It featured some of the treasures they found too. When it was finished, Ella asked how the treasure had got there in the first place and who had put it there.

The Lieutenant Governor explained that during the Second World War Germany had occupied many countries including France and they took some of the art treasures from places like the Louvre, not only wanting them for themselves but also wanting to keep them from being damaged or destroyed. Jersey was a good place to hide the treasure; it was free from bombing by the allies and was close by, being a short crossing over the sea. The military hospital built underground provided the perfect hideaway. The Germans would have brought the treasures over by sea from France and a few trusted men would have been involved in securing the treasure, so that it could be safely hidden away until the end of the war. These were most probably the SS. The thing was Germany did not win the war so the treasure was lost until now; thankfully, it remained safely stashed away.

"What will you do with it?" asked James.

"The treasure belongs to the Crown, but for the moment, it is staying with the Jersey Heritage who will take great care of it. Some items will be returned to the museums and art galleries they came from and the rest initially will go on tour as the Nazi treasure found on Jersey. After that it could well be sold off and the money will go to Jersey Heritage," said the Lieutenant Governor.

"That reminds me," he continued, "being such gallant treasure hunters you will all receive an award. You will each get £10,000."

"That is very generous of you, sir," said Marcus. "We actually thought there may be a reward and we discussed what we would like to do, we are very grateful, but we wish to put that money into building a Physic Garden here on Jersey so everyone can benefit from it."

"What a fabulous idea," said the Lieutenant Governor's wife excitedly. "A Physic Garden, yes, and we can get people to help maintain it and it will, as you rightly say, be for everyone to appreciate nature at its best."

Ella looked at Maud who winked at her as she was sitting in her wheelchair beaming.

"That is a very generous offer and one which we will certainly take you up on," said the Lieutenant Governor. "Thank you."

As the adults moved into the dining room for their lunch, Ella said to Marcus, "Just tell me what a Physic garden is?"

Marcus explained it was nothing new; hundreds of years ago, people had Physic Gardens. They essentially contained herbs and medicinal plants. James added he had visited a Physic Garden in Cowbridge in Wales, near where his grandparents lived. He said it looked much like any other garden except the plants and flowers were all naturally or organically grown and it was beautifully set out so that people could sit and relax amongst the plants and enjoy the beauty of the garden.

"I was told we had to give something back," said Marcus. "This is something that every one of us can enjoy and it is part of nature so I think Annabel or Titania or whatever you want to call her will be well pleased."

Ella smiled. "I think it will be great and hope that I can come back and see it next year."

They joined their parents and family for lunch in the Governor's House and what a splendid lunch it was too.

As they left later that afternoon, the children walked to the gate and there in front of them was a large horse chestnut tree with its spreading branches. There leaning against the trunk was a beautiful lady. Her long blond hair floating down over her shoulders and her dress had a fine beige pattern which seemed to camouflage her with the tree trunk. Her eyes sparkled and she gave them a beaming smile. Her left hand touched her lips and she blew them a kiss. Marcus and Ella smiled. Then just as suddenly as she had appeared, she melted away. James was not sure what was going on and wasn't sure either if he had seen anything at all.

The very Reverend Michael Hambly and his wife lived almost next door and they invited everyone in for a drink. Grandpa and the parents wanted to see Lillie Langtry's grave so Michael said he would be only too happy to show them. They disappeared into the churchyard saying they would join the others later.

Jenny, Art, Maud and the children went with Vivian back to the vicarage. They had a splendid garden and after they had all been given a cold drink, they sat around chatting. The children then had a chance to speak to Maud who was just so delighted that she had been able to have lunch in the

Governor's House. Maud beckoned to Ella who bent down to her.

"Did you see her?" she asked. Ella knew she was speaking about the Faerie Queen.

"Yes," she said.

"The Physic Garden is a wonderful idea and I hope I live long enough to see it."

"Of course, you will, Maud," said Ella smiling.

Vivian assured the children that she would organise a trust fund for the Physic Garden so that the public could have life membership for £50 and the money would go to maintaining the garden. She thought it was a splendid idea and looked forward to helping to set everything up.

Later that evening back at Spud End, Tom, Ella's brother, told her he thought she was crazy.

"You were offered £10,000," he said, "and you have put it towards some poxy garden, you need your head looked at."

Ella ignored him; she knew she had done the right thing.

It took a whole year for the garden to be planned out and created and Ella and her family were invited over to open it to the public. Initially, the children were asked to do the honours, but it was Ella who said she felt there was someone else that would be more appropriate.

Ella asked Maud if she would do it and at 94 years of age, she said she would be delighted. She refused to use her wheelchair and after cutting the ribbon and officially opening it, she walked around supported on Art's arm and viewed the splendid arrangements of plants and foliage. She stopped at times and made use of the seats that were placed around the garden. The centre point was a splendid fountain with orangey carp swimming around beneath it in a large oval shape basin, which also held beautiful white water lilies.

Ella stood back and felt pleased with what they had achieved. Vivian and the Governor's wife had worked hard organising it all and although the garden looked in some places quite bare, she knew that in a few years it would be absolutely amazing. As she watched, she noticed an elderly couple standing by the fountain, an old man with white hair and spectacles sitting on his nose and a little old lady with a funny cloche hat. They were looking at her and smiling. Ella smiled back, this time not feeling the least bit scared. In an instant, they seemed to disappear. There were two drops in the water and two carp swam vigorously away. Ella closed her eyes. "Did I really see that," she said to herself. *Time to find Jenny*, she thought and went to join her by the large stone sundial.

Would you have taken the GBP 10,000 or given it away as Ella did for a garden?

Why do you think James was unsure about seeing the Faerie Queen?

Do you think Ella was right to let Maud open the Physic Garden?

Physic Gardens are very special, do you think we should have more in our neighbourhoods?